Pailin – Blood and Fire

Nguyen Van Hong

Translated into English by Hanoi Female Translators

Ukiyoto Publishing

All global publishing rights are held by

Ukiyoto Publishing

Published in 2023

Content Copyright © Nguyen Van Hong

ISBN 9789360164584

All rights reserved.
No part of this publication may be reproduced, transmitted, or stored in a retrieval system, in any form by any means, electronic, mechanical, photocopying, recording or otherwise, without the prior permission of the publisher.

The moral rights of the author have been asserted.

This is a work of fiction. Names, characters, businesses, places, events, locales, and incidents are either the products of the author's imagination or used in a fictitious manner. Any resemblance to actual persons, living or dead, or actual events is purely coincidental.

This book is sold subject to the condition that it shall not by way of trade or otherwise, be lent, resold, hired out or otherwise circulated, without the publisher's prior consent, in any form of binding or cover other than that in which it is published.

www.ukiyoto.com

Contents

Chapter 1	1
Chapter 2	9
Chapter 3	26
Chapter 4	35
Chapter 5	47
Chapter 6	58
Chapter 7	69
Chapter 8	75
Chapter 9	82
Chapter 10	87
Chapter 11	98
Chapter 12	110
Chapter 13	117
Chapter 14	123
Chapter 15	135
Chapter 16	142
Chapter 17	152
Chapter 18	160
Chapter 19	170
Chapter 20	177
Chapter 21	189
Chapter 22	198
Chapter 23	204

Chapter 24	212
Chapter 25	215
About the Author	*229*

Chapter 1

The four-seat, black Toyota Camry left Bat Tam Bang town to Highway 5, straight towards Phnom Penh, the capital. Under the Pol Pot government, the road suffered many injuries, filled with potholes since it had never been repaired, the cars did not drive as fast as the pedestrians; Now, the road surface is widened for four lanes, smoothly asphalted. Phearak just hold on the number 4, let the car rush, even when crossing the bridge, he did not need to slow down, feeling lightheaded as if he were walking on clouds. Chi Tai sitting in the co-driver's seat sometimes had to remind:

\-   Please be careful, Phearak. Not only the two of us, but also the mother and daughter sitting in the back...

\-   You can rest assured, I've been driving for nearly twenty years, never made a mistake. At night, the road is empty, don't worry!

\-   I believe in your skill, but who knows, in decades, it only takes a small mistake for a moment to pay the price!

\-   You see, whenever a car appears from afar, people rush to both sides of the road, sometimes at night I don't need to "flash", during the day there is no need to honk, the road is vast, there are few people and cars 100 or 120km/h speed is more than comfortable!

Phearak is quite skilled because he has been a car assistant since he was just over ten years old, running the Bat Tam Bang - Phnom Penh route. In addition, the density of people and vehicles on the road is currently sparse, now he has his very own car and is the owner of a business, Phearak drives himself to work every day.

- More than 300 kilometers, about ten o'clock in the evening and we will arrive to Phnom Penh! - Chi Tai aided and took off his seat belt, leaning back on the chair while behind Phearak's wife and daughter leaning against each other and nodding.

The car passed through the town of Muong R'Xay at only 19:30, they stopped by the roadside, went to the toilet before nightfall, the car continued to drive under the moonlight at the beginning of the week. Soon the town of Cong Pong Ch'Nang appeared, sparkling in the shimmering, colorful electric lights. Out of town, Chi Tai pointed to a few tanks lying on the side, some tens of meters away from the road and said to his sworn brother Phearak:

- When the Vietnamese volunteer troops flooded into the capital Phnom Penh, the remnants of Pol Pot fled here, set up a defensive line, and drastically prevented the pursuit of the Vietnamese army and the Cambodian revolutionary armed forces. Nearly a dozen tanks of the Vietnam-Cambodia coalition were burned here. It's dark now, but during the day you can see the burnt-out T54 scattered on both sides of the road!

Phearak clutched the steering wheel while rolling his eyes to the sides and front, he tried to picture the tanks lined up horizontally, across the clearings and sparse woods, the black muzzles spewing out red bullets, hitting the remnants like ants, running for their lives on 5th Street, then spilled into the western jungles without a trace.

- I was born after the Vietnamese volunteer troops withdrew from the country, so it is difficult to understand the fight on this road. The remnants of Pol Pot's soldiers both stopped and fled before the stormy attack of the volunteer army and the Cambodian revolutionary army. Before fleeing, they destroyed all bridges, culverts, houses and temples on all over the road from the capital to Bat Tam Bang town. The Lam River army volunteered to chase them to Lech, Ta Sanh, and Pailin near the border of Thailand, then stopped. When the Central Highlands Army went to Cao Me Lai, they "threw" his unit into the middle of the "land of life and death" like a "stone" falling in the middle of a hornet's nest. Oh Pailin! It's been decades, every time I think about it, I get goosebumps!

- I haven't traveled much, but I've heard people say that Pol Pot has caused fields of death, and human bones piled up like mountains; everywhere I go, I see skulls baring their teeth and rolling their eyes. It's terrible. Why do they kill people so easily? In the past, in Cambodia, the dead were not buried but burned, they put the ashes in jars and brought them to the temple. Perhaps, during the years under Pol Pot's rule, too many people died and could not be burned, so there were piles of bones like that!...

- During the years of international duty, I went through almost all the provinces in the West of Cambodia, it's the same everywhere!

As the two men kept their conversation going, the car came to the capital's center at any time. It is now 22:45. The streets are busy, and people and cars are intertwined under the yellow street lights. However, in the shops, restaurants, bars, the lights are flashing, the drums and music can still be heard from miles away. Phearak dropped his soul into the traditional Khmer music, he drove while whistling. The Toyota Camry was like a bright dot, sucked into the capital's starry sky.

- We will go to Thang Loi Hotel right away. If we arrive at the time guests are already asleep, we will bother them, or maybe we will lose the opportunity! - Phearak seems impatient.

- I think so too. If Buddha does not "bless" us today, there is no hope for another time!

Following the instructions of the beautiful receptionist, the four entered the elevator to the 5th floor of the 5-star hotel building, standing in front of room 505, Chi Tai still retains the natural look of an experienced person, but Phearak's chest was pounding like never before, he had to lean back against the wall to let Chi Tai knock on the door. Chi Tai had to knock for the second time, he raised his hand to look at the watch, it's 23:00 o'clock. It looks like the guest is already in bed. After the "click" sound like the person inside pushed the door latch, a beam of light shot out directly at Chi Tai and Phearak. Not letting guests have to speak first, Chi Tai politely:

- Hello sir, my name is Chi Tai, sorry to bother you. "Are you Uncle Hung?".
- Yes, it's me, Hung. Nguyen Mong Hung. What's going on? Please come inside!

The guest named Hung, rolled his eyes and looked around: a young man named Chi Tai, a tall man with short hair, Southern accent, looked like a Viet Kieu (overseas Vietnamese). In the capital of Phnom Penh, there are quite a lot of Viet Kieu of Southern origin, this person has a pale skin like a soldier who has weathered rain and sun. The other guy is unmistakably Cambodian, big and strong, with a full face, ruddy, toned, about 1m62 tall, 29-30 years old. The woman with honey skin, wearing a sarong with beautiful curves and a girl about 5-7 years old, probably his wife and children. Mong Hung, with a gentle appearance, spoke as if encouraging:

- Come on, you guys have something to say. I'm listening!

- Sir, before coming here, we had contact with Vietnamese tours agencies. We want to find a man, thirty years ago, he commanded a regiment to protect Pailin, a town to the West of Bat Tam Bang town. In recent years, whenever there is a group of Vietnamese tourists traveling to Cambodia, we paid a visit, but there's still no luck. Yesterday, we were in Siem Reap, tonight, from Bat Tam Bang town, we came here when hearing that a delegation was in the capital Phnom Penh. Please help us, let us know about the person we are looking for! - Chi Tai asked Phearak to take out a black and white picture, size 13cmx18cm from his pocket. Phearak does not know Vietnamese, Chi Tai points to each person on the picture:

- The person wearing this black glasses (the right hand rests on the shoulder of the woman whose face looks like a statue of a dancer in the Absara dance, the other hand hangs down) is Ngo Xuan Manh, one of the 5 commanders to fight in defense of Pailin. The woman sitting next to him lived in Sang Ke. Both are Phearak's parents - Chi Tai pointed at his sworn brother. And here is his wife and children. Since birth, Phearak has not known his father's face. His mother passed away. He wishes to see his father's face, even once in his life. He is working for a travel agency. If you know, just tell him. He is 30 years old this year and has a wife and two children. This is the first daughter! - Chi Tai presented on behalf of Phearak, then he said about himself: "We are sworn brothers. After completing the international mission to return home, I found his situation pitiful, so I found a way to return to this mortal land to help him".

Mong Hung didn't say anything, flipped the photo over and over under the LED light, the room was brighter than day, looked closely at each of the two's faces, and then raised the picture higher, tilted his head as if he was thinking about something. Looking at the back of the photo, his silvery eyebrows are drawn close together; Wrinkles dilated and folded like ripples on a bald forehead almost a third of the head. He smirked, half-smiling: "Rats desert a falling house (!). Mong Hung did not expect a commander in front of the enemy has full courage and wisdom, but in front of a woman, he "falls" so easily? Then he thought about the years of fierce fighting, seemingly impossible, how many of his comrades had to lie down forever, incarnating into the blood-red soil in a place thousands of kilometers far from his country. Where would this country go in that war if there were no Cambodians in the back as their fulcrum? In a "water fish" relationship, sometimes the sexual instinct breaks all barriers of law, national boundaries, nationality and even hatred between people. What we need to cherish today is the unhesitating sacrifice of the soldiers. Ngo Xuan Manh is an example. Looking at the old soldier's face, sometimes thinking, sometimes beaming, Phearak's mood is like a person holding his breath to cross the river, both worried and hopeful in a man worthy of his father's age. He raised his head and said:

-       You have found the right address, the right person to look for. I will help you and hope that one day Phearak will meet his dear father and respected grandfather again! - Mong Hung said to Phearak and turned to Chi Tai: "This will take time, because I only know Ngo Xuan Manh through the picture is exactly a volunteer soldier. As for the address, he just wrote on the back as NT. In my opinion: NT can be an abbreviation of one of the 60 provinces of Vietnam, and each province has many districts and communes, looking for a person is like finding a needle in the seabed. I will go through the Veterans' Associations to find out where he is...

Chi Tai and Phearak, joy and happiness are evident on their faces. To bring pride to the Phearak couple about their Vietnamese-blooded father, and also to once more Mong Hung show respect and admiration for the stalwart officers and soldiers of the past on the Pailin front, and maybe this is the main purpose. He said:

- It's already late at night, tomorrow my group will return to Saigon, if you ask, I will stay here for an extra day to tell you about the Regiment that Phearak's father was the commander during his years of international service. Together with Cambodian troops and people, he overthrew the genocidal regime of Pol Pot, bringing the country back to life!

- Yes, thank you. Well then, there's nothing better than that! - Phearak and Chi Tai were as happy as saying at the same time.

Chapter 2

In the 25-30 square meters 5-stars standard room, fully equipped with high-end facilities, in the capital Phnom Penh, Phearak and Chi Tai listened attentively as if swallowing every single word from Mong Hung, talking about the Regiment led by Ngo Xuan Manh. Phearak rarely heard a sentence, maybe it was because he was self-studying Vietnamese under the guidance of Chi Tai, while his wife and daughter just listened but didn't understand at all. Chi Tai appeared to be an insider because he had been lying and suffering on the land of Pailin for many years.

- Did you know? - Mong Hung opened by commenting on the strengths of the west of Bat Tam Bang town. Pailin was once a busy town, like a commercial city and a famous tourist destination when Cambodia was in its "golden age". Economically, it is home to rich and diverse natural resources, mainly diamonds and forest products. The land here is basalt, suitable for industrial crops, especially coffee and rubber. When the "Buddhist armies" (Vietnamese volunteers) first came here, there were many warehouses for storing coffee beans and drying yards covered in cement. In the ruined neighborhoods, you see cold stone mills and discarded coffee grinders piled up. Under the Pol Pot regime, Cambodians were prohibited from using the products they made, mainly for export abroad. Regarding security and defense, Pailin is an outpost, a strategic fortress to protect Bat Tam Bang town in particular and nearly half of Cambodia against invasion. One of the advantages is that Pailin town is located in the middle of three roads: Highway 10 from Bat Tam Bang, Route 58 from the north and the road from Thailand. Around the town are high mountains and dense forests, which are very convenient for deploying troops. Here is also a place to trade with countries in the region through Thailand and then into Cambodia. Because of its location, it became the target of enemies in the past and even after the fall of the Pol Pot government. Since the day Ngo Xuan Manh's regiment was stationed here, most of the remnants of Pol Pot were mobilized to gather around this ruined town to retake Pailin to be the "capital of the resistance" for the government that has collapsed. They have to live in exile abroad, so it can be said: the war situation here is extremely fierce.

Did you know? In the rainy season of 1983, Pol Pot soldiers launched many attacks on Pailin town in all three directions: the east, they cut off traffic, destroyed bridges, and made it impossible for us to resupply. In the north, they followed Route 58 to attack with many fighting forces inland, raiding targets around Bat Tam Bang town. In the west and southwest, they relied on the mountainous terrain close to our base, planted mines, and ambushed with firepower.

The infirmary of the Vietnamese volunteer infantry regiment was often overloaded. Injured soldiers are returning increasingly, mainly because of landmines, wounds from the waist down, and many have to amputate both legs. The morgue is also full, some cases have to be taken to hammocks, hanging under the trees, waiting for moving. Looking at the number of wounded and dead soldiers, one can know what percentage is due to mines, straight bullets and other reasons. Also, we learned the enemy's plots and tricks and what strategy should be applied to cope. For a whole month, there was no train up. Route 58 from the north is muddy, walking is already tricky, only motor vehicles can run in the dry season. 2 bridges were destroyed on Route 10, the arterial road from Bat Tam Bang town, east to Pailin.

Regiment commander Ngo Xuan Manh ordered the 3rd Battalion standing at Cau Chay, by all means, to clear Route 10 down to Pang Ro Lin, and contact the 196 Division of Mr. Coi Bun Tha, Cambodia soldier. But it could not be solved overnight. Invalid and dead soldiers still had to lie there, waiting like forever; there was no way to move.

For three or four years, several divisions of Pol Pot's soldiers, from the Eastern and Northeastern fronts, surrounded Pailin. Our soldiers met them everywhere, it also meant we got ambushed and stepped on mines.

\- I disagree when saying that this is just a "remnant!" - Regiment commander Ngo Xuan Manh strongly opposed that view in conferences.

\- If it's not a "remnant", what do you call it? - The front-line Commander narrowed his eyes and looked directly into Xuan Manh's face.

\- Commander! In our previous offensive campaigns, the enemy fled to preserve their forces, then they quickly regrouped, fully equipped with bases along the border. So they can't be called "remnants" but are combat units! - Manh knows he need to convince the Commander.

Around this small town, their main divisions encircle the 3rd Regiment. Three years pass slowly, the clock seems to stop, the Regiment led by Xuan Manh still stands firmly, thousands of kilometers away from his rear, in extremely harsh climate conditions. Malaria, tuberculosis, dysentery, and malnutrition… are chronic diseases here. Pailin is the focus of the fever epidemic in Southeast Asia. However, at no time did regiment commander Manh and political commissar Tuyen ask for reinforcements. Up to this point, not a single soldier has returned to the rear without returning to the front. Now, Manh feels stuck. He did not have the strength to handle unexpected situations. The enemy pressure around this town was increasing day by day. They had just established a firebase on the height of 321, able to control the entire north area of Pailin, it stood there as if challenging a regiment of volunteer infantry in the distant land full of traps. The danger of losing Pailin is looming, a critical, strategically important target in the west of Bat Tam Bang, where Son Sen and Ta Mok have been boldly marked on the battle map for the past few years. They hoped to cut off two transport routes related to the survival of the Vietnamese Regiment: Route 58 from the North, Route 10 from the East, combined with local pressure to force the opponent to withdraw Pailin. Reowning Pailin will bring the Central Office here as the capital of the resistance after losing Cambodia.

For the first time, Manh "raises his hand" to ask for help from his superiors, Pailin's survival is now not only a risk, but the lives of hundreds of people in this town are also being decided day by day... Thinking over and over, Regiment commander Ngo Xuan Manh called the forward command post:

- I only ask for help with the number of seriously injured and dead soldiers, they can't stay here forever!...

The Regiment commander was upset and frustrated when he received a response from the headquarters:

- Comrade! Please organize the force to clear Route 10 smoothly. We will send a car!

- If Route 10 has been cleared, we don't even need a car - After saying that, Xuan Manh hung up the phone to express his dissatisfaction at the request of the superior. He thought that the radio communication network reported wounded and dead soldiers daily. The increase in casualties means that the number of combat troops is reduced, and the higher authorities must also know how much the fighting strength of this 3rd Regiment is still. The fate of this town needs more attention. Manh did not require the mobile forces of his superiors to relieve the enemy's pressure that was weighing on his Regiment. Wouldn't the officers and soldiers of a regiment who once roamed across the South Central battlefield during the years of anti-Americanism in Vietnam would give up before an opponent who was formerly our student, now there is no place left on this front. During the years of the resistance war against the US, the British Regiment was like an independent unit, operating in the area of Zone 6. In those years, there were many difficulties, hardships and fierce battles, the military zone only set out a policy, all Thrilling issues took place in battle, all of them resolved by themselves, never showing signs of dependence on their superiors. After the liberation of the South and the reunification of the country, the Regiment had just started doing business when the border war occurred while almost all the facilities for fighting were nothing but hoes and shovels, and the fighting force also "Running while queuing". The situation of the Regiment now compared to then, although not entirely favorable, is not satisfactory.

- This time is the end of the rainy season, the enemy is taking advantage of the weather to strengthen the attack, causing more difficulties for us. The rainy season has many disadvantages. Soldiers raided the forest, malaria increased, and food sources were not supplied due to the separation of transportation routes. However, the situation still needed to be to the point of requiring the mobile force of the superiors. The high number of casualties is partly due to the poor technique of detecting and detecting enemy mines...

Faced with the complications that arose, the regiment commander made a preliminary assessment of the situation during an extraordinary meeting of the Regiment's party committee. According to him, the current difficulty is "seasonal difficulty". In any rainy season, the enemy has conditions to promote his forte in guerrilla warfare. Their conspiracies and tricks are nothing new. But it must also be recognized that our troops have not really adapted to a strange battlefield and the characteristics and nature of a new war.

The Regiment commander continued:

- I suggest some points, comrades. First, we must firmly take the initiative to attack, break the current stalemate that the enemy is getting closer and closer to our base, but we refuse to come out. Second, to lower the casualty rate from enemy mines while hunting. Finally, encourage the soldiers to take advantage of local materials to increase the quality of their daily meals while the transport road is "clogged", the rear has not been able to resupply!

The Regiment commander's points could have been more popular, Xuan Manh realized, it seemed to be entangled with something in the few people sitting in front of him...

- Mr. Manh's opinion is very true to the current situation of our regiment! - Secretary Binh voiced an adjunct. Too high casualties, raging malaria. However, the cause part is important!...

Binh also paused for a moment, looking sharply at the officers in front of him as if to judge from their eyes, who agreed, who opposed. He continued:

- Talking about the form of defense. If it is a defensive battle, it is necessary to attach importance to the construction of solid fortifications and to arrange tight obstacles. We must rely on fortifications and hindrances to fight the enemy. At the same time, we also rely on them to preserve our forces. One of the reasons leading to high casualties is enemy mines because we focused too much on chasing the enemy in the terrain. Whatever the target, if we get out of the fortification without armor, the only way is to die! We must rely on fortifications and trenches, clinging to them and fighting until the dry season. The dry season is unfavorable for the enemy, but it is the "business" season for us. At that time, we will wipe out their bases along the border. Their guerrilla war will be over!... Seeing people around silently listening, thinking they agree, as if encouraged, Binh continued: "It's been almost a month now, wounded soldiers have increased, medicine was almost running out, we had to use reserve drugs for "plan B". I suggest limiting sending the troops out. Just roaming around the mountains and forests, not only getting hit by mines but also being healthy!... I asked the logistics agency to check the storage, too see how much we have left: rice, food, instant noodles... We need an output plan for the units, prioritizing the forces on the front line. Here, in this abandoned town, there is nothing in the locals to take advantage of. Otherwise, it will violate the forbidden rules of the front!... Yesterday, I saw a few guardsmen bring back all kinds of things: papaya, mango, jackfruit, and milkweed. Sometimes I still hear the sound of explosions in the stream. Fishing? There are only a few puddles of water, not that much fish to catch. The current military discipline situation is worrying. We should reduce the number of meals to prolong the waiting time behind the resupply than to let the troops violate the rules. Comrades, we must remember "discipline is the strength of the army". A unit that violates discipline will have no combat power. I tell the truth, I will punish whoever that person is!... I have sent agency officials to check and heard that some comrades are digging for diamonds and rubies, waiting to exchange cigarettes and goods downtown. We came here to help them overcome the genocidal regime, help them rebuild the government and armed forces, not to do those things. We stand here to protect this town, comrades. We must understand that we are protecting the homeland from afar!..." - Binh said more enthusiastically, without being tired. It seems that many things that have been pent up since Binh came here, now he have the opportunity to unfold like a spring:

- The current situation of our regiment is worrying, our combat strength is seriously reduced, if not saying paralyzed. I suggest reporting up front honestly so that they might come up with a serious plan. In the immediate future, it is required to send a mobile force here to relieve Pailin and be ready to deal with enemy attacks!...

The whole meeting room seemed to suffocate, everyone looked at each other in bewilderment. The officers here are also insiders, fighting with the enemy, and have tasted all the bitter, sweet, challenging, arduous and deprived years of the past. However, they do not think the situation has yet to reach a bad level as assessed by Secretary Binh. However, they still felt secure and believed in the commanding ability of Regiment Commander Xuan Manh. Once he told them: "I am still here, comrades, rest assured. We live and die together!" Now, the secretary's opinion seems to contradict. But it is not only the assessment of the enemy, the policies and measures are inconsistent. One side requested to send forces outside the base to take the initiative to attack the enemy; another side must cling to fortifications, rely on fortifications to preserve their troops. The Regiment commander's policy is to use local materials and increase the quality of meals to improve the squad's health. The political commissar's measure is to reduce the amount of daily meals to prolong the waiting time behind the resupply, to strictly abide by the regulations of the front on the battlefield. The Regiment commander considered it unnecessary to use the division's reserve force, so the political commissar asked to bring up the mobile workforce immediately... The conflicting opinions are also thorny issues that need to be resolved. So the meeting became more lively. At the end of the meeting room, the 2nd battalion commander nudged the 1st battalion politician in the ribs.

- What do you think?
- The commissar is partly correct. In the rainy season, sending forces to hunt outside is not appropriate. If we stick to the fortifications, arrange obstacles around and combine with good firepower, they won't dare to come here anymore. It is advisable to use local materials to increase the quality of meals when we need help in terms of food. In this abandoned town, besides papayas, green mangoes, water spinach, crabs, and skinny shrimp, what else is worth more? When not used, these fruits ripen and fall to the ground; the shrimp, the starving fish, rot and pollute the scarce water we are using. In combat, we collect from the enemy to improve our forces, which has been summed up as a guideline! This is the political commissar a bit mechanical, his "occupational disease". Now it is impossible to implement the "only use dry firewood, spring water and air to breathe" regulation like the early stage of the Southwest border war! - He also recalled the story "monkey" that everyone in the division heard at that time: "Do you remember, the whole 1st Regiment Command was warned just because a monkey was discovered sitting on the shoulder of a regimental cadre on the way to attack the enemy. The monkey was always amused, grinning while the whole 1st Regiment command board had to sit down to review, their face were as pale as if they had just had their household registration cut off!... And now, it would be strange if a monkey was

sitting on a tree in front of me, like fat in front of a cat's mouth, without giving him a "copper candy" to put him in the pot, it would be strange, and only the people in the Wildlife Protecting Committee in Europe just returned the monkey to the forest!"...

- I'm the complete opposite of you!
- Does that mean you're on the side of the Regiment commander?
- Not a fact, talking about the point of view, the perception of the problems we are facing. Blood-related matters need to be said seriously!
- We're having a serious discussion, then!
- Seriously, you brought the monkey thing in here!
- Oh, you still don't know about the monkey?
- I know, but don't bring it up here! - What the two battalion cadres meant when they argued and looked at Secretary Truong Thanh Binh...

Outside, it was raining heavily. The mountain winds from the East blow up the valley with no way out, bouncing back and hitting the tin roof. Both sides of the Regiment commander Xuan Manh's temples twitched. He did not expect his opinion to be rejected mercilessly. Since the day political commissar Tuyen went to a supplementary class in Hanoi, his superiors sent Truong Thanh Binh down to replace him. The idea that Binh is the support and the center of solidarity in the entire Party Committee, at least in the trio of Standing Party Committees of the regiment, hopes that Binh will increase his determination and energy to overcome, together take responsibility. Xuan Manh was surprised and disappointed by Binh's argument. He did not ask for a compromise. No need. Usually, in some units, to maintain internal unity, sometimes people have to be patient with each other, and keep quiet, because of the precious harmony, so as not to affect those around, even though the two sides have opposing views. If it is elsewhere, they will clash fiercely, even swearing to death.

The regiment commander gulped several times, trying to push down his emotions. It seemed like a thorn kept lying in his throat, making his eyes watery, his poker-face facing the door, the sky seemed to darken. He thought: so far, Binh has been sitting in the office forever. When the South Western border broke out, he was assigned to the units as an inspector, detecting and correcting discipline violations by the troops. Like the officer in the North, he directly disciplined people and teams, regardless of their rank and position in the "territory" he managed. At that time, the inspectors had great power and authority. Many cadres lost their rank, their positions, and at least received warnings like the "monkey case", most of which were discovered from officials doing inspection work. A soldier was dragged to be shot at the front because he violated the civil discipline in the newly liberated area. It's just a matter of necessity. Now Binh's role is no longer in the strong position of an inspector. Still, as a secretary, a regimental commissar, he has the advantage of defending his point of view. Truong Thanh Binh is from the Central region, one or two years older than Xuan Manh, a cadre from a basic background. Unlike the Regiment Commander, in conferences, the secretary talks too much. When Binh spoke, he did not care about the whispers and gossip.

Above, the speaker kept saying, below, even a few guys were playing or sleeping, he also let it go. Someone said that the secretary has no self-respect, right or wrong, if people listen to him, he must also listen to what they say. This is a weakness of the commander, also is the personality of Truong Thanh Binh. Because of that, Binh doesn't know if his subordinates agree or disagree, but he only believes in what he gives as a philosophy. His career way kept "coming up". From an assistant, through years of smooth work, Binh jumped to the position of secretary, political commissar of the regiment, never once had any contact with reality. What helped him fulfill his responsibilities as a cadre were mainly "given opportunities" after several short training sessions. Such people are often stereotyped, mechanical, and will-only, they will defend their opinions to the end (!). From these thoughts about Binh, Xuan Manh said that he did not hold any grudge against, only his work situation that created such a model person.

Suppressing Binh's unconvincing opinions, Regiment commander Manh stood up and slowly presented his point of view. As an enthusiastic and dynamic person who has been through school, mainly experienced in actual combat, at first Xuan Manh also spoke softly and briefly, but later on, his heart beat faster and faster as if there is a lump in his throat:

-In my opinion, whether fighting offensively or defending, we must fully show the thought of attacking the enemy. In defense, the idea of attack must be put on top, and must combine three factors to create combat power: fortifications, firepower and mobile forces. This mobile force means to defeat the enemy from afar, not passively waiting for them to come. If you just stick to the fortification, sometimes the fortification becomes a grave to bury yourself! Sorry!...

Thinking that he was exaggerating, especially against the secretary's opinion, Xuan Manh seemed to regret it, but after only a few seconds, he regained his composure, because he believed in what he said. "I should use softer and more humble words (!)". He thought to himself and continued:

-Speaking of declining health and high casualties due to the deployment of forces to chase the enemy outside, that is also what we are trying to overcome in order to minimize casualties, but still have to step up the fight, don't let them stick around, which can easily lead to the risk of losing the latch. Pailin has the highest density of mines per square kilometer of any war zone in the world. However, every difficulty has solutions. Suppose we do not boldly go beyond the base to fight the enemy from afar. In that case, they will cling to and surround our base and plant mines right in front of the cellar door, in the kitchen and even under our bed. I'm asking you, my comrades, to resolutely send forces outside to find the enemy, destroy them, and boldly block them right from the starting point. I am the highest commander here, I will take all responsibility to my superiors!...

The last words of the Regiment commander made the atmosphere of the meeting tenser. Everyone thinks that this tension lies in two people, the two highest here are the regiment commander and the political commissar, it arises from two points of view. Binh sat there with a cold face. He had to admit that what Xuan Manh said was true, coherent, and convincing. Binh sees his reason is not right, not suitable. He was angry with himself, angry for his hasty, talkative but immature. Binh tried to overcome this inherent habit of his forever but could not. Instead, just keep quiet, listen. In folklore, there is a saying "A wise man speaks in the middle of a conversation". As the chairperson of the meeting, he should only listen and take notes of everyone's opinions and then draw conclusions based on that emerged as a keen secretary. Unfortunately, he wanted his voice to be bolder and heavier in the party committee's resolution, because he was the secretary, but unfortunately his military knowledge was unfamiliar in this regiment.

Usually, when a resolution has been issued, that is, the secretary's draft presented to the collective to dissect, analyze and vote with over two-thirds, sometimes 100%, the secretary has fulfilled part of his responsibilities. Later, if the resolution is not followed properly, in order to fail for the unit, the head must take responsibility. When listening to regiment commander Xuan Manh say: "I am the commander, I will be responsible to my superiors!", Secretary Binh nodded his head. Afraid that people around him would think that he was challenging the regiment commander, so after nodding his head, Binh still shook his thighs, his feet pounding on the floor like he was in harmony with a music. What happens in the future, it's good to say nothing, if the situation is bad, for example, the enemy captures the post, the soldiers encounter landmines, cross the border, and the investigation is lost, the cause is still the same due to the organizational stage, failure to comply with the resolutions of the Party Committee, subjective command, loss of vigilance, loose management allowing the soldiers to violate discipline, etc..., As in the case of high casualties due to sending forces to hunt down the enemy outside the base, Binh should have had to stick to the fortifications to preserve the force until the dry season...

The meeting dispersed. Cadres and party members left with two views from the two chairmen. And then in the regiment also formed, very naturally and unknowingly, two factions, two views... It remained dormant for quite a long time. When the regiment's situation had symptoms, it revealed that all activities of this unit on the Pailin front had been halted...

Chapter 3

The rainy season has not decreased but fiercer. Looking up, Pailin's sky was like a giant cast iron pan upside down, it seemed that you could touch it with your hand. Fog covered the mountain slopes. Visibility was reduced to less than ten meters. Pouring rain. Bubbles of water burst from the sky and ran onto the ground. Water flows along the roads, sweeping away all the garbage that fills the sewers. These are the last rains of the season.

For more than a month now, all attempts by the reactionary government to win on the battlefield to put on the international conference table have failed. At Pol Pot's headquarters, Son Sen presented his battle plan before the end of the rainy season.

- Our 519th Division in Dang Kum is facing the 5th Division of the Vietnamese army. In the past four years, our troops have encountered it at Ampin, at Cao Me Lai, at Poi Pet... The 179th Division of Mr. Hun Sen, commanded by General Ho Xa Won, Military Region 4, stands at Sisophon. There is a rumor that it will replace the 5th Division. Recently, our scouts reported that the Vietnamese and Cambodian commanders went up and down in this area. They must be preparing to hand over each other!...

Defense Minister Son Sen gave a stick to draw an arc along the North-Northwest border of Cambodia. He paused to think if there was anything more to say in this direction.

- This direction! - Son Sen continued: they determined the main direction, so they gathered two divisions with vital equipment!... - He sneered: "What do we need, mainly or secondary? We'll do the opposite!" With that said, he left hanging, and turned in another direction, the direction that all efforts in this rainy season must capture Pailin.

- In this direction! - Son Sen also drew an arc from South Cao Me Lai to Ta Sanh - they also had two divisions. The Vietnamese Division was spread over hundreds of kilometers. Their formation is very scattered, there is a lot of space. Our scouts know very well that we can attack whenever we want and bring in as many forces as we want. General Coi Buntha's 196th Division is gathering at 10th Street, in the future will go to Pailin to switch to a Vietnamese Regiment currently surrounded and isolated by us. We have encountered this regiment in the area of Muong R'xay district, in Cao Me Lai, in Ba Van and Route 10. However, they are in trouble in Pailin now. We must focus on hitting harder. We still advocate avoiding clashes with Hun Sen's troops. For now, the Cambodians don't fight the Cambodians, we will talk to them later. Attacking the Vietnamese army to deepen the contradictions in their so-called "Combat Alliance"... Determined to cut off Route 10, not allowing a convoy of trucks to enter Pailin. There must be ambush fire on all the airstrips when their helicopters land, keeping the air under control!

Ta Mok seems to have ants crawling behind his back, standing still. He was known as a reckless and brutal commander. Every place called a "hot spot" appeared a man with short legs, jumping like a wolf with a leg missing. He has escaped many dangerous situations. The limp leg was the cause in a near-death experience due to a collision with the enemy. Ta Mok impatiently waited, but his superiors refused to stop. He stood up and snatched the words:

-       In order to capture Pailin, there must be close coordination on all fronts! - The Chief of the General Staff narrowed his eyes at Minister Ieng Sari, the head of the diplomatic front. We must take advantage of the international community's support and continue to condemn and force Vietnam to withdraw its troops from Cambodia. I agree with Mr. Son Sen, we need to focus on fighting the Vietnamese army. This plan is very wise, this psychological attack is perilous. Currently, there is a battalion of Vietnamese troops standing at high point 107 on Route 58. This battalion is standing there probably to rescue Pailin from the north. If this goal is not excluded, it will be very difficult to capture Pailin, because from there, it only takes a few hours to walk to Pailin. A second target that cannot be ignored is Route 10. In this direction, in addition to the 196th Division, there is also a Vietnamese battalion located at the east of Pailin. We will combine fighting with besieging this battalion, forcing them to "stand still"... If we can do that, their forces in Pailin can't handle it, they have to withdraw like before. You guys remember? In 1979, we lost Cao Melai, then tried very hard to push them out of that sacred forest, poisonous water!

Son Sen cut Ta Mok's words:

- Capturing Pailin is difficult, but once you get it back, it's good to keep it. There I know, the architectural works of a city are very suitable for wartime, economy combined with national defense. Underneath the two or three-story buildings, there are underground tanks for rainwater, enough to last for months if under siege. The drainage system is also trenches run along the roads leading to the town center. The coffee plantation has been abandoned for a long time and can be very well hidden. We will lay mines, set traps on the roads, every corner of the house, and every square meter of land in this valley. Guerrilla warfare will grow to its peak, burying the enemy all over this town!...

Ta Mok continued:

- There is also a great advantage of being connected to the Southwest front. From Pailin down to Co Cong to Xihanouk Vill port is a very dangerous area. We rely on it to receive foreign aid and bring it to the warehouse. Pailin will be the resistance capital!

Ieng Sari was annoyed by listening to the crowd chattering about the not-so-bright prospect, especially when Ta Mok was tampered with. However, he seemed to be still a bit sober:

- That's what you said, but we have many disadvantages. Previously, a mighty army, tanks, cannons, planes, and warships could not hold the capital Phnom Penh, now it's all gone, and there's no strength left to get it back. I attended a meeting at the United Nations, I know, the support of the international community for us is much smaller than before! In terms of military knowledge, I am more ignorant than you. Still, in my opinion, we need to strengthen our forces to build a strong base at point 321, to prevent the enemy from attacking along Route 58 from the North, and to be the springboard to capture Pailin when the time comes. If I get the town back, it will be mainly for shelter in the short term. Then it will count!...

When "tea after drinking" in the base in the murky, remote place of the Pailin mountains, Ieng Sari sadly said to Son Sen:

- In this government, no one is more intimate than between you and me! We were both born on the land where we should have spent our lives so our children and grandchildren could be a little proud of their ancestors. In Tra Vinh, I have many close relatives. Many of my classmates used to be there. Now that they know about me, they probably hate me very much. Unfortunately, I have gone too far from my ancestors and my race, and now it is too late to repent. Indeed, we will never be able to return to that place of birth, not even once!... - As Foreign Minister, Ieng Sary gets to go to many meetings, so he grasps the world situation, follows a logical course, he realizes the fatal mistake for himself and for the reactionary government in pursuing the most bizarre way of building a regime in human history.

Son Sen knew that the Minister of Foreign Affairs was telling the truth, he added:

Sometimes I think just the same way! Why should I leave that place, where fish and shrimp are full of rivers and fields, to come to this country? Is it because of a political career? Perhaps due to the wild spontaneity of rebellious youth, I have abolished the nature of those born on that swampy ground and become their enemies of the place that brings us the ladder of fame for today!...

- Hey! - suddenly, Ieng Sari moved closer to Son Sen, lowered his voice, and spoke softly enough for two people to hear. You need to be careful! There are signs that the prime minister is trying to get rid of you!... - Ieng Sari doesn't want to say this, after all, he and Pol Pot have a "family relationship" and are "comrades-in-arms", but because of his brother's rudeness, he couldn't stand it. Many times Son Sen also sensed that, and he also thought of how to cope if such a dire situation happened:

- Me and Ta Mok are in charge of national defense! We often rely on each other. You already know Ta Mok. He also did not like the Prime Minister, the conflict between him and the prime minister was intense. In this government, the Prime Minister doesn't care about anyone. Then at some point, he will take the risk!...

Ieng Sari sadly looked up at the map hanging on the wall in a newly built house in the forest upstream of the Sang Ke River, nearly a kilometer from the Thai border, in the North is a continuous old forest to Pailin. As a construction site, Thai people are exploiting timber and minerals. Thinking for a moment, the head of the diplomatic service stepped closer to the map and raised his glasses:

- The high point 321 has a critical position compared to the whole area! - He raised the stick in a semicircle, embracing the northern part of Pailin town. This area is within range of direct fire, and rainbow fire and it can reach the center of town. There is no better position! However, if it belongs to the other party, it is also very detrimental to us. Therefore, whether we like it or not, we must be determined to keep it! Why is such a significant position left open by the enemy? Or do they have a plan? We must be careful or we will make mistakes again!...

They all sat listening, getting goosebumps thinking: if the enemy can jump to that high point, the entire base and treasure in the West got nowhere to move... Then how to ensure that the area is "inviolable".

- Follow me! - The Chief made a plan again. We will prepare two plans: One is to place 321 as a fortress, turning it into a grave for the "Duon" people right around the hillside. Second, there needs to be a plan to make sure it stands up to that function!...

The meeting to discuss their plans at the forward headquarters lasted until noon and still needed to be finished. Everyone can see the powerful high point, significant in a meaningful way, determining Pailin's existence. The main thing now is how to protect it, to ensure it can take advantage of the terrain when the war occurs here.

- The center of the coffee plantation has a 105 mm artillery position, along with other fire systems, if they intend to attack, our troops will not be able to stand it! - Ta Mok is the "old fox" commander. He's been on all fronts. He knew with the enemy's way of fighting, they called it "Army Contract Raid", if it happened, they would have no chance of survival, no matter what the high point was, so he determined to return to the traditional fighting method applied from the beginning of the war until now. However, the country had fallen into the hands of the Hun Sen government, it had caused the "foreign army" to suffer and be bogged down in this war. He believes that the motto "The enemy advances, we retreat; The enemy retreats, we pursue" is still valid and consistent with the defeated army's position and strength. He concluded:

- If a fortress is built here, it must be built according to the motto that has been applied so far. That means being flexible!...

When it comes to "command to guide the operation", you here have already understood. Only then can the existence of the exploding government-in-exile can be prolonged.

- How to protect that "fortress"? - Ta Mok exhaled, exhausted from talking too much. A force must be deployed here! - He pointed to a point on Highway 58 about 3 km to the North with the name boldly printed on the map: Salak'rao. The Chief of the General Staff concluded the final plan: Salak'rao - 321 - Com Rieng, forming a tripod base cluster. It's ideal! That is the only way to rely on each other to disperse the enemy's forces. If Vietnam attacks base 321, they can't help but consider the other two bases!...

Chapter 4

Receiving orders from the battalion assigned by Captain Tung, Tran Duy Chien commanded the squad to cross Route 10, to the area of Pang Ro Lin, a place about 3 to 4 kilometers from Pailin town. The enemies often come up to plant mines and ambush there. The squad consisted of five people, each carrying 3-day food. This area does not have to worry about water shortage because there is Sang Ke River, named after a district nearby. Anyone can reduce the cost of carrying a bamboo tube, only a flask is needed to wear in belt.

Today, Chien feels worried. If the situation is bad, losing one still has someone to carry, how to handle two? Working away from the unit, there is no communication device, how to report to the headquarter? Chien begs the Captain in a melancholy Quang Nam's accent:

- Captain, I want to ask for two more people, just in case...

- Don't you ever think about bad luck! This year, we were not allowed to add more troops - Chien knew that the Captain would say the same, but he still asked. Captain Tung needs clarification, not knowing how to use his forces, the scope of responsibility is broad, but the number of troops is too small. Tomorrow there is a helicopter, and he has to send his forces to South and North directions on Route 10. The Captain softens his voice:

- Well, you try, I knew it...

Chien keeps himself silent. He was worried because last night, he heard an owl call in the east as if foreshadowing something at one o'clock in the morning. Chien didn't tell anyone. He could only pray for this trip.

Early in the morning, before departing, Chien told Chinh, his best friend had many good memories from the first days of wearing a soldier's uniform until now:

- Chinh! Take this book for me. If anything happens, bring it back to my mother. This is a diary I wrote from the day I stepped out of the house. My whole life was in it. I love my mother so much! I have a reputation as the oldest brother, but I have not been able to take care of my mother and younger siblings. When I was a child, I made my mother suffer all sorts of things. Growing up, I felt a little responsibility, but then I have to leave for this...

Chien was born crying in the roar of bombs and bullets. His hometown Quang Nam was covered by the fire and smoke of war. As his father died early, his mother worked hard to raise the children in a poor condition. His mother used to say: "In this house, you are like no other. If you're good, try to equal others!".

Mother scolded Chien every time he asked to join the army. Chien said to his mother: "If you are wiser than your father, you have a blessed family!" Chien rarely speaks, his face is always thoughtful and vague, as if he is full of ambitions in his head. When he was sitting on the school chair, he often told his friends when he saw them arguing:

- I wouldn't say I like the habit of saying things that don't go anywhere. Let your mind think of more useful things!

A girl agrees with Chien:

- That's my type! Girls could be loud, but boys shouldn't! - This saying of the girlfriend is the starting place for the school age with childish romantic.

The sound of gunfire began over the border area, Tran Duy Chien got away from his mother's arms, and stepped into the car, but his heart was still attached as if something was holding his legs. Chien was present on the southwestern border and joined the volunteer army to go on an international mission in Cambodia. Chien handed the diary to Chinh. The diary was crumpled, tinged with Pailin red soil, turning the pages to yellow.

- Don't think too hard! This trip will be good! - Chinh took the notebook in his hand, glanced at the cover to put in his backpack, but then handed it back to Chien. Keep writing! I don't know how to write a diary. And remember to write it all down, including us in it. In a way or another, our squad still has some alive to come back and tell everyone the stories later!...

- This notebook is running out of pages. Yesterday, I had to temporarily write in the cigarette case, when I buy a new one, I will copy it! - Chien was afraid that his teammates would misunderstand him, so he clarified: "Don't think that I am nervous. In combat, anything is possible. I'm just expecting all scenarios to be ready. You see, not only can we take risks, but our company of dozens of men, our whole battalion, our Regiment has been around this valley every day with losses, but no one gives up. Just imagine we're going to the hardest place today!..."

Chien and Chinh were walking and talking when a person in front turned around and waved. All four pairs of eyes looked up to follow the index finger of the leader of the formation. Chien hid behind a tree, Chinh sat down behind a termite mound. They all looked at each other's faces, then looked ahead, silent. The sound of howling birds mixed with sad cicadas in the distance echoed, signaling the coming of summer. The woodpecker on the other side of the stream knocked for a long time, the mosquitoes went to find a human ear to bite. In the sound of rustling leaves, and murmuring water coming from below, a young deer bewilderedly stepped into the stream, just lowered his head to drink a few sips of water, looked up and suddenly saw Chien, he jumped on the shore in a panic, run away into the forest. After a while, there was the sound of landmines exploding...

- He hit a landmine! Poor thing, I don't know if he's alive or dead? - Chien whispered. The whole squad continued to search along the stream, going up to Sam Lot, south of the diamond quarry. The old primeval forest, the stumps of two or three people hugging, thick woven leaves above each other, jostling each other for light, below the tangled vines wrapped around the legs. A python with a diameter of up to the palm of an adult's arm, the middle part swells up like a ball, lying motionless. Maybe a pig or a roe deer is in there. When he was a child at home, Chien heard people say that when a python swallows the prey, like a pig, it lies still for several months, and thatch grass grows through its body and covers it like a clump of reeds. When the prey in its stomach was exhausted, the python got up, climbed up the fork on the tree, head down, and all the prey's bones fell to the ground. It is said that in the Tonle Sap area, Siem Reap has the python furnaces of local people. Chien plans to buy a few ounces when he has the opportunity. The doctors said: python is more suitable for women, when men use it a lot, they will become infertile... Remembering that, Chien thought: If you stay here forever, every part of your body will become paralyzed (!)...

Thinking about the python, Chien missed his step and fell into a deep hole. This forest has many pits because people exploited diamonds and precious stones in the past. Currently, on the upstream Thai people are exploiting. The excavated rock is put into a wire mesh sieve, using a pump to discharge water onto the sieve, the sand is washed away, revealing iridescent diamonds of different sizes. Because of that, the water is always turbid downstream of the Sang Ke River. Pol Pot is allowing foreigners to exploit timber and diamonds in this area to have money to prolong the agony of the reactionary government that has no place for stability. Chien thought: "Diamonds are nowhere to be seen, only mines".

Chien struggled forever under the deep hole, Chinh walking ahead, did not look back, nor did he hear Chien call. Thinking that the squad leader was going to the toilet, Chinh stopped for a while to wait until he listened to a tiny voice, he ran over and pulled Chien up. Fortunately, the hole is deep, but after each rainy season, it is slightly accreted, now the shallowest place is only about one and a half meters. The more you go upstream, the steeper it becomes, everyone has to carefully trace each step, peering at each tree, and grouping rocks as if looking for something.

-This area is close to the place where forest products are exploited. There will be many mines for sure! - Chien reminded the squad to be careful.

The squad leader led the brothers up a small stream from where Pailin flowed down, the water was clear. This is the contiguous area between two volunteer army units, the North is the range of the 3rd Regiment, the South is the 25th Infantry Regiment. Adjacent places often have loopholes. That may be why today Tran Duy Chien's squad is the first to set foot here.

There was a girl's squealing ahead. The whole squad sat in place, not moving. Captain Chien crawled forward. Everyone put their fingers on the trigger and waited. Chien chose a high place, and secretly raised the binoculars to observe. Chien's two fingers adjust the sharpness of the binoculars. A waterfall appeared, about 10 meters high, pouring water down with white foam below a puddle like a small swimming pool. The three girls' bodies are like three plaster statues struggling and playing in the clear water. Two people were looking up at the waterfall, hair falling to their shoulders, one turned to the front, showing clearly in the binoculars a round, sparkling breast. "Oh my God! Why are there so many beautiful flowers in the middle of the vast mountains and forests? - Chien stammered. The water reached waist level, reflecting the naked bodies of the three girls. The girls play freely, with all kinds of poses. One of the girls lying on her back, spreading her legs wide, her arms floating on the water... Chien waved his teammates:

- Hey, come up here and see!...

The binoculars were passed to the whole squad so that everyone could admire the girls' pearly bodies, to enjoy the rare moments for soldiers on the front, who had known only guns and mountains for years in a foggy forest without a female figure on the very edge of the deep border of this country, moments that awaken the vitality of youth that have just passed over the years. Many people have forgotten that they are men. While his teammates were taking turns watching,

Chien immediately thought of his Hoi An girlfriend, who he had not seen for more than a year, wonder what she is doing now? Chien recalls X…, his ex-girlfriend with similar personalities, was in the same class. She sat at the front desk, Chien was in the back. Because of the naughty nature of the school age, he always remembered his "excessive" action toward her. That day, while the teacher was lecturing, X… leaned back against the desk, her hair swore on Chien's notebook. With Cuu Long ink bottle on the table, Chien put a lock of X hair… into it. When X… stood up to speak, she pulled her ink-stained hair, painted a heart-shaped on her shirt. Of course, X… did not notice. In the afternoon, she used a brush with soap to rub the fabric until it was torn, but still couldn't remove the ink-stained. That ao dai had to be abandoned. That memory will probably follow Chien for the rest of his life. The day he broke up with his lover, she leaned her head in Chien's chest and cried. Chien kissed on her hair, the smell of locust mixed with the smell of a girl made him ecstatic. An invisible force is so strong, pulling between those who stay and those who go. At night, Chien could not sleep. In his restless sleep, the image of a girlfriend wearing a white Ao Dai, with two braids bearing the mark of school age tied by two red strings, then passionate kisses, salty because of tears showing up…

Someone stepped on a stone, causing it to fall from the bank to the streambed. All three girls were startled and stared at Chien and his teammates… One girl squealed in horror. All three girls rushed ashore, grabbed their clothes, and ran away. One girl held her shirts, but leaving her pants, one girl pulled the pants hooked to the tree branches, stood naked, ran up a slope, and disappeared into the forest... All the guys blankly looked at the silhouettes of the girls.

\-   Indeed, there is an enemy base on the stream! - Chien said.

Mr. Ngoc whispered just enough for two people to hear:

\-   Maybe not the Pol Pot base but the Thai people. I heard the Pol Pot has sent Thai people to exploit timber and diamonds in this area. Perhaps girls are Thai who come here to serve the bosses!...

- We should get out of here. If the people know, the Pol Pot will know!

Tran Duy Chien sent the squad back. They walked but their heads kept turning to look in the direction they ran, as if regretting a rare opportunity... The old forest was still quiet, containing risks. The sun slanted to the west, the afternoon sunlight penetrated the foliage, sending fan-shaped light trails to the ground. The murmuring stream of water is heard in the distance, mixing with the eclectic sounds of the majestic mountains. Walking under the shade of trees, a light speckled like hundreds of thousands of moonflowers in the quiet countryside. The soldiers filled their chests with the fresh afternoon air. Chien led the squad in the direction of the deer earlier and it may have been hit by a mine.

There was a loud bang at the bottom of the stream, near where the girls bathed under the waterfall. The explosion sound hit the cliff, and bounced back, reverberating with the wind. Chien whispered to himself:

- If we leave that place a little late...

Ngoc, who was walking behind, said:

- Indeed, at the top of that stream is the enemy base. The girls ran up and shouted that's why they hit down here!

- Maybe it was Pol Pot's force protecting the mining people. The girls are prostitutes who come here to "entertain". I've seen in nude pictures before, Thai girls are so pretty!

A comrade followed jubilantly:

- If we could secretly approach to "borrow" a girl for fun!

- When I was in school, I had a beautiful girlfriend. We knew each other so well that I can control her as I wanted... Now I still feel sorry for missing such a "strategic opportunity"!

The story of the girls kept buzzing until the platoon leader reminded:

- We must pay attention, this forest is near Route 10, so beware of mines!

On the road there is the sound of cars. Today, Chien's squad went down to sweep the south of Route

10 to ensure the safety of the vehicles going to Pailin. There are forces on the North of the road. Whenever a car boarded up or a helicopter landed, the 3rd Regiment had to organize a security operation. The two sides of the road must be thoroughly searched, the engineer must carry the machine to detect every meter of land to see if there's any mine burrow. What a bunch of dumb ass. The road security forces were only withdrawn after the last truck loaded up, and turned around.

For two days now, Chien's platoon soldiers have eaten dried rice. The dried rice soaked in the water of the Sang Ke River, it swelled, mushy, and pale. How to cook boiling water here? Chien had a stomach ache again, his stomach rumbling in waves, making his face grimace. Everyone expected the convoy to return to the unit, climb into the hammock and take a nap to make up for the past few days.

Hoping to finish the mission this afternoon, in the rumbling of the convoy returning, a loud bang, shook the ground, startled the leaves out of the branches and fall around... The battalion of Chien nearby ran up. Two anti-tank mines overlapped, the GMC'ss driver sitting in the cabin was bounced back, causing his head to flatten, and he died on the spot, the blood flowed down to a red pool under the car... So Chien's squad had to stay and guard. It is really dangerous here at night, the enemy can sneak in to attack. Darkness quickly covered the forest. Frogs begin to play the eternal music of love when it's mating season. Rats pulled together for late-night snacks. Chien's teammates each occupied a tree stump and sat there for the rest of the long cold night of the Pailin border region to watch over the vehicle and a martyr. The night rain sprinkled on the wet clothes. Chien sat there, looking at the darkness, his heart filled with remembrance of his mother, of his brothers and sisters, of the noisy, bustling neighborhood next to the small market; He missed the atmosphere at night under the dim street lights, shimmering in the roaring waves of the sea. In the house in the middle of the shabby neighborhood, everyone is probably sitting in front of the TV watching a football game or movie. Mommy! Tonight I am sitting under a cold tree before the muzzles of the enemy. Did you know your son…

Chapter 5

Divisional political commissar Nguyen Van Chuc turned each page, the lines were blurred, dancing before his eyes. The writer's zigzag handwriting was difficult to read, and he had to judge both ideas and intentions, his eyes were cloudy, flashing under the glasses, his forehead was broad, and his kind face showed many wrinkles. The Executive Party Committee of the division received a report on the situation of the 3rd Regiment sent by Secretary Truong Thanh Binh this morning. Looking at the letter, the commissar could only sleep from evening now. It was midnight, and he sat contemplatively by an oil lamp. "Has the Pailin Front reached such a critical point?". Every day, during the briefing, he did not listen to the report. Regiment commander Ngo Xuan Manh called up and only asked to transfer the number of wounded and dead soldiers to the rear. The rest of the activities are still going as planned, without support.

In addition to the general situation report, political commissar Nguyen Van Chuc carefully read and reviewed the attached letter of Secretary Binh, reflecting some more issues that need to be rectified. Binh said: the main cause of high casualties is the application of inappropriate tactics. The soldiers were out in the woods all day, wearing wet clothes for a week, and colds and malaria increased. The most serious is organizing forces to cross the border, one soldier is missing (suspected of being captured by the enemy or illegally crossing the border). The discipline situation of the soldiers is also a matter of concern due to the lack of persistent handling, the decrease in the trust of subordinates towards their superiors, and many other problems... The Secretary of the Divisional Party Committee sensed that something unsettled had arisen between regiment commander Manh and political commissar Binh. Political Commissar Chuc said that Binh has yet to experience reality. Still, in terms of party and political work, he has experience detecting situations, like a weather forecaster, when the sea is calm, they can sense the approaching storm...

In recent years, the Executive Committee of the Divisional Party highly appreciated the leadership ability and organization to perform the tasks of the Party Committee and the commander of the 3rd Regiment. Is there anywhere on the Northwestern front and even in the lands of several provinces of the 479 front the Vietnamese Volunteer Army took on more decisive responsibility than Pailin? The most severe malaria is also there. However, not a single officer or soldier of the Regiment gave up their combat positions or abandoned their duties to go back. At the Northeastern front, the 3rd Regiment was the unit that completed the task excellently when the 1st Regiment was penetrating deep in the 1st squadron and was searching in the rear when "it" bravely rushed in front of the battle formation. The same cadres, since moving to the Northwestern front, were assigned the task of defending Pailin, facing many difficulties and challenges, the Regiment still stood like a rock, never once asking for a mechanical force. From the day he set foot in Chua Thap, perhaps "it" was the only Regiment that eliminated a Battalion of Pol Pot troops, not a single one escaped in Muong R'xay district. Our soldiers used to reduce their daily rations to save the hungry people of our country, go to the deep forest to bring people back to their old hometown, help people build houses, bridge bridges, make roads, build schools, hospitals... and many other beautiful jobs. The places where the 3rd Regiment passed through all left an indelible good mark in the hearts of the Cambodian people about the image of a volunteer soldier on the international battlefield,... light... "This guy just came down and discovered many problems (!)". In a leadership team, the role of each individual is vital. From that inference, political commissar Chuc was satisfied when he sent Binh to temporarily replace Mr. Tuyen to attend school. If the situation of the 3rd Regiment is exactly as Binh reflects, he can be left there in the future.

The town of Pailin is surrounded by the enemy, but it is Ngo Xuan Manh, the regimental commander who is fighting to protect this town, is also surrounded on all sides... On the battlefield, his heart aches when every day, every hour, the soldiers fall, the list of wounded soldiers grows longer, the cemetery next to Bat Tam Bang airport adds many new graves... for which he is the first to be responsible. In the rear, as a husband and father, he cannot remain indifferent to the situation that his wife has no job, cannot afford medical treatment for his children, have to leave the countryside to go to the city. Every hour, every minute, they are waiting for him. Another attack on the position of a regiment commander was no less malicious. Those are the conflicts arising from the person who should have been spiritual support, giving him more strength, not to mention having to shoulder the burden and share with him in difficult times. In addition to the wrong views of the political commissar in the assessment of the regiment's situation, recently Binh also secretly wrote a letter to the Executive Party Committee of the upper level to protest, not aimed at anyone other than regiment commander Xuan Manh, brought the troops out of the fortifications, causing high casualties, increased malaria; Which is the subordinate who violated the nine provisions of the front but did not take disciplinary action. The most painful thing is allowing the troops to cross the border to "bring the war to a third country, " which negatively impacts diplomacy... Recently, Xuan Manh also heard the news that shocked him; it's from Binh that He connected with some people in the rear, including his wife, and organized for some people to go up Pailin to cross the border to Thailand... Binh sent assistants to check to verify and collect evidence. If so, then the political life of this regiment commander will be destroyed... Every attack seems cruel, but Secretary Binh's attack is the most dangerous and drastic...

As a lively, outspoken but cautious person, Regiment commander Manh still considers Binh upright. Binh has no personal enmity. Manh said: what's the point of getting angry? It is even more inappropriate to say that it's a competition because Binh is a political cadre, the rank is equivalent, but he's the head of the regiment's party. All individuals and organizations must submit to the leadership of the Party while Binh is the secretary. In Xuan Manh's mind, due to his distorted and ignorant views on military knowledge, he has not been experienced in reality because he was not properly educated, which has turned him into a mechanical, dogmatic man and somewhat "confident" because he does not know his ignorance. Unfortunately, if not verified or thoroughly considered, all the problems reported by a cadre like Binh damaged the Party, some key positions were shaken and even ruined his career... So many troubles came to Xuan Manh at the same time. He was pessimistic, depressed, and surrendered to fate. But then, he thought of his responsibility as a Regiment Commander at this ruined town with thousands of lives. Xuan Manh tries to get rid of all the troubles so that his mind is always sober.

- If necessary, you can discuss with Mr. Manh to adjust the formation to fit the actual situation! As for the army's ideology, it is necessary to calmly look at it objectively, avoid haste when there is no collective conclusion. We must consider the actual situation at each moment to see the essence of the problem!

Before the delegation of agency cadres was sent to check the situation in the 3rd regiment, the divisional political commissar suggested issues to consider before the inconsistent assessment in the standing party committee of the regiment that Secretary Binh had asked. Nguyen Van Chuc is a sharp political cadre, sensitive in all matters, with extensive experience in party work, political work, and handling rational and emotional relationships. People like him are often cautious in their words and actions. He said that the situation in Pailin recently became complicated after Mr. Tuyen went to school. Still, it may have yet to reach the level as Binh said. Binh is unfamiliar with the work in a combat unit and has not yet grasped the basic concepts of military thinking. Learning the situation in the combat unit differs from the office; could it be because he was too nervous? If you are in a hurry, you often see things that tend to be subjective.

The helicopter rode to the front carrying wounded soldiers, food, and military medicine; sitting in the front was a group of officers sent by the division headquarters to reinforce Pailin. Usually, before landing at the landing site, the pilot circled around Pailin's sky to see a town in the middle of a deep green forest with trees and flowers under the bright sunshine of the tropics. Located less than 10 km from the border with Thailand, Pailin is the western gateway to Bat Tam Bang town. Rows of two- and three-story houses along the streets are designed in the "Western", "Chinese" style close to both sides of the motorway. Traces of restaurants, hotels, bars, shops, nightclubs, casinos, temples... are still left in ruins caused by the ravages of war and the draconian policy of the genocidal regime. . Peace, this place may be a tourist-commercial-service area of Cambodia, coffee and rubber production and processing farms, diamond and gem mining and refining factories will spring up in this valley. Today, the pilot broke that habit, not "walking" in the sky of Pailin, but from a distance of more than three thousand meters, flying up and down Route 10 and landing directly on the landing area. Perhaps the pilot was affected by the "unique" flight over Siem Reap a few days earlier. That day, from the airport, the HUIA took the deputy commander of the front and a combat officer to inspect the northern mountains of Siem Reap province. The helicopter circled a closed circle over the airspace of Angkor Thom, Angkor Wat. The five towers of Angkor Temple appeared amid deep green trees passing under the plane's belly. The pilot raised the altitude and widened the circle to embrace the Cu Len mountain range. A cottage appeared under the palm tree forest. "This area has no people, why are there houses? Pot's base (?)". The plane had passed quite a distance, at the direction of the deputy commander, the pilot pulled the lever to the right, tilted the wing, lowered the altitude, and was hit by a barrage of 12-7 bullets from below. A "lost" bullet entered the engine compartment, after going through the jaw, broke the teeth of the combat officer, who refused to stop there, the shot continued to enter the aircraft engine and broke it. The deputy commander quickly put his hand over the faucet. While controlling the plane, the pilot just communicated with the ground and gently landed at Siem Reap airport... There were drops of sweat on everyone's face. A suffocating situation like a circus show, only the mortal soldiers on the battlefield did not panic. Not to repeat this situation, the pilot let the plane land in the "emergency landing" mode today. A transport platoon was waiting, bent down from the tree line to carry the goods to the warehouse. They seem to be doing well. The parcels from the plane are brought down, and someone picks up and takes them away immediately. The enhanced officers also jumped down and quickly went back to work. Then wounded and sick soldiers were brought up to fill their seats on the cabin. The plane's engine echoed in the distance, reverberating against the cliff above the screams of the loading commander.

Around the landing area, mushroom-shaped smokestacks appeared. Explosions also mixed with the sound of aircraft engines, but someone recognized the explosion of 82mm mortar shells, shouting loudly:

- The enemy bombarded the airfield!... All dispersed!...

Three corners of the landing area hit three bullets. One bomb exploded about 50 meters away from the plane, many of them falling to the edge of the forest in front. The pilot did not hear, he reached out and pulled the door to listen to the rattle. The propellers increased rotation, lifting the plane slowly off the ground. The aircraft tilted its wings, made a half-turn in the sky above Pailin, said goodbye to the soldiers on the ground, and disappeared behind the distant mountain. Only then did people hear the sound of mortar shells continuing to explode around. For a moment, everything was in order, as quiet as here, there had never been an enemy mortar shelling.

Regiment commander Xuan Manh paled and ordered the battalion commander of the 3rd battalion to go to the headquarters. In the local combat plan, the 3rd Battalion in the Cau Chay area, east of Pailin town, the 1st Battalion north of the coffee plantation, must have forces outside the base daily, scouring the area. A square kilometer between the two units to eliminate the enemy close, clinging around. However, a mortar field has been set up here, waiting for the helicopter to land, pouring dozens of shells on the landing area.

- This morning, if the helicopter was hit, what would you say!... - Regiment Commander Manh shouted in front of the two battalion commanders. The two battalion commanders' faces were stained with pity.

- Chief, discipline us! We are exhausted. This morning I sent two teams to that area, but less than two hundred meters out of the base, they were hit by mines, and had to carry each other back on stretchers. There's no one left to go on!...

- Are you challenging me, comrade? If the plane caught fire, how would I discipline you properly? Can your lives be exchanged for dozens of wounded soldiers?!...

Chief of Staff Thanh added:

- I announced a flight two days ago, and you refused to release forces to let the enemy plant mines close to the base. They have followed your path, and your steps, and planted mines right from the starting point, only a few hundred meters from their battlefield!

The Chief of Staff turned his eyes to the 2nd battalion commander:

- Same in your direction. Less than a kilometer from Cau Sap to pole 505 but you keep letting them hit; I saw that the soldiers had a phenomenon of shrinking into the cave like a hedgehog recently!...

Political Commissar Binh sat quietly with his head on the desk to record and take notes. He realized the fatal mistake of opposing the regiment commander's plan to launch people to fight the enemy outside the base. Binh knew that this resulted from being entrenched in the fortifications, not daring to escape to fight the enemy from afar, the enemy was close to planting mines around, the mortar battle was also at a dangerous distance. As the regimental commander said, maybe he will plant mines in front of the cellar door, in the kitchen and even under the bed...

Xuan Manh wanted to say something more to prove that the point of attack against the enemy in defensive combat was applied on the Cambodian battlefield. But, after the opinion of Chief of Staff Thanh and the fleeting gestures on the political commissar's face, Manh thought: maybe he has noticed, so stop... This morning's briefing was a warning, a reminder those who are protecting Pailin day and night that: the enemy is still there and right next to us, they will not leave us alone, the vital future of this ruined town rests on our shoulders...

Chapter 6

This morning, Chien's platoon stepped up to replace the force at High Point 505. This front post is very thorny, not only because it is both high and steep, but also in the middle of the border. On the border marker, the East side shows the words, no longer clear and sharp - "CAMBODIA". Opposite the other side is THAILAND. Knowing that, there is no need to come up here to hold. This landmark was built during the French colonial period. This area of Southeast Asia is using maps printed by the French at that time as a standard for territorial disputes. So, why bother with arguments, just follow the map and recognize each other's sovereignty.

Anyone can think that simple, but in a world still in chaos, a landmark, no matter what reinforced concrete is cast, is nothing. In this world, everything is created by human hands, if it can be built, it can also be destroyed, there have been many milestones between countries that have been moved back and forth by inch of land. Even in the field, two landowners also encroached on, and encroached again. On this High Point 505, there is only one squad, sometimes only one platoon, but it does an enormous task, protecting Pailin town, contributing to the complete defense of the territory of Cambodia. Tran Duy Chien wrote a letter to his mother: "I stand here, although thousands of kilometers away from my hometown, although at the end of your country, we determine that: fighting the enemy here as above. his country; I'm standing here to protect my motherland." If in 1979, the Vietnamese volunteers had not saved the Cambodian people from genocide and then pushed them to this border area, they would probably have been close to the vicinity of Saigon. No one with a conscience can forget the tragedy of the Vietnamese people massacred along the border in 1977. Now, the front posts like the 505 that Tran Duy Chien's squad stood on are necessary, no could be otherwise. And the volunteer soldiers standing here still can't be with them...

The late-season rains drain off any remaining water before the dry season arrives. Although the dry season is equally harsh, it is the "business season" of the people protecting this sacred land day and night. The rain gradually receded into the night, the day was dry. The official dry season is when no drop of water is left in the sky. The lead-colored dark clouds gradually faded and turned to white light, swept by the wind to a faraway place, at the end of the horizon, the space seemed wide and airy. The cicadas put on their thin coats and perched on the trees, chirping. Sparrows and parrots chirped, calling each other to find fruit trees. In those forests, soldiers from both sides spread out, looking for each other to solve the "debt" in the struggle in the land of life and death, which takes place on each road, each ruined neighborhood for many years has consumed a lot of blood and blood but still can't be defeated... The trails in the early morning, the red soil is still thick, sticking to the feet, until noon is dry. Gradually turned into dust, red basalt dust like blood stained the trees on both sides of the road. It takes a little sharp eye to detect someone's traces on the road, in the groves, on the lawn because of the remaining night dew.

Living in a harsh environment due to natural disasters and artificial disasters, people must be cunning, must be slick, it is a survival instinct, not only in humans but also in all plants and animals on this planet. that feature. Less than 300 meters away, Chien's squad discovered and removed two mines. The first fruit was left under the bumpy brick, coming down from the steps of the dilapidated house, with the eyes of experienced people, Chien doubted the brick as if someone had brought it and had just put it down. He gently flipped the brick over, and the "hidden man" revealed his proper form as a green mine. Since when has "Death" been waiting here? This is a "detonating" mine, only "begging" for one foot. Chien neutralized the landmine and put it in the bag like a person collecting scrap.

- Mines surrounding, you have to pay attention! - Chien reminds those who are behind and then continues to move forward. Now they are more vigilant. It was cold in the morning, but there were drops of sweat on their faces. Is it possible that the moments of tension between life and death left on Chien's face not only sweat mixed with basalt dust, but also more and more wrinkles on his forehead, making him look older than twenty years old, the age is full of life? Ho Ngoc was the one who discovered the second landmine. He said:

- This mine, if planted before the rain at night, is difficult to detect. Maybe they're just hanging around somewhere. The camouflage soil is new, leaving footprints on the side of the road!

- This is the area near the station. A little further away, there may be more mines! - Mr. Chinh followed Ngoc to add ideas to make people pay more attention. But squad leader Tran Duy Chien thought differently:

- Not really! The enemy planted mines so close to the campsite like this because we didn't spread out to search around, it kept getting close, both damaging us from the starting point and giving their forces outside the freedom to circle around after raiding. The further away from the garrison area, the fewer mines may be deployed. Where did they get the mines and scatter them in the mountains?!

More than 10 o'clock in the afternoon, Chien's squad reached the top of the slope at the foot of High Point 505. Here there is a stream, a cement bridge from ancient times has collapsed, and soldiers here named this area "Cau Sap", below the clear water flowing toward South-North. The whole squad stopped to shower and cook lunch. This peg, change troops once a week. After a week, another force came up instead, they came down here to retake a bath. When going to the post, each person must bring 20 liters of water, each day can only use up to three liters, regardless of level, rank and position. At the bottom of this stream, they bathe and dive as much as they like. Water poured down from above, heard the rattling, white foam. The two sides of this stream is where a unit is stationed, so it's safe, except in the case of a distance, somewhere they "threw mortar fire" down here. But don't be afraid, on peg 505 there is full firepower to shoot straight, shoot rainbows, put bullets down to respond. The winds carried water vapor, flowing along the streambed, and Chien felt that his soul was too peaceful.

While waiting for the rice cooker to cook, Chien sat on a large rock near the stream bed, took out a notebook to keep a diary. It is true that "the scene becomes poetry", but with Chien, he can write poetry at any time, even when he sleeps talking nonsense is also poetry. When you see his confused face is when the form of the poem and will spread out on the page. Chien still kept the habit of keeping a diary from the moment he entered the soldier's life, taking off his vinyl shirt, putting his slim body into a withered grass-colored military uniform, baggy like a country woman wearing "one-piece pants" ". In the lame squad larger than the "tam tam" group, only Chinh and Ngoc were naughty, curious to know what Chien wrote about Hoi An's girlfriend in the other diary, but also only recently, at the end of the second episode of Chien. Chien's poems were written on the march, between two battles, when going to hunt down the enemy in the vast forest, and even during each meal and sleep on the post. The soldier's poems, though heavily smelled of gunpowder, but whether the girls are "sluggish" or "narrow-minded, selfish," if seen, please have a handkerchief ready to wipe your tears... Now Sitting on a stone in the middle of a stream, with a little longer time, Chien made a few poems for the dreamer:

I write to you in the middle of this world / Pailin - the border, day and night rain / I write to you at noon / The fire and smoke of the battlefield smells of praise...

Chien looked up into the distance, from the depths of his soul as if appearing in front of the Hoi An girl, in a student's long dress, two braids swaying in the morning sun, running to find her at the farewell ceremony from the homeland of Quang Nam. He remembered the memories at school, leaving a stain on the student's ao dai that his heart both loved and regretted. Then Chien thought about his mother. Oh, what are you doing now, maybe you're dropping your tears thinking about your son at the far end of the border. "Mom, don't be sad. Please stay alive and wait for your son to return (!)…".

While reliving with memories of his hometown, and mother were always the source of inspiration, most talked about by Chien in the diary, when the rice cooker was cooked and was brought up on a flat stone like a tabletop.

- The water is scarce at the pinnacle, if you give rice and sesame salt, water iss never enough. I have calculated each person can bring up twenty liters, use one liter along the way, use three liters per day for cooking, drinking, and personal hygiene. 7 days a week, the cost is twenty-one liters!

While eating, Chien "accounted" for the amount of water brought to the peg. One guy added:

- What about water for watering vegetables to fulfill the company's target of green vegetables?...

- - Irrigate vegetables, take advantage of water to wash rice and dishwashing liquid! Ah, I forgot, water for the Barracuda, he must be thirsty!...

Ngoc and Chinh are the two most enthusiastic person in the squad, sharing their voices:

- Let's count twenty-one liters!

On the day of sweeping the remnants of enemy troops in the west of Muong R'xay district, a southern district of Bat Tam Bang province, while crossing the mass burial pits caused by Pol Pot soldiers, a bird's nest was blown by wind and rain, fall off from the branch, the two young birds were still red, bewilderedly raised their necks, opened their mouths to ask for food. Chien is heartbroken when thinking about the children playing with the flow of life because their parents were killed... Not ignoring them to let the rain and wind blow, Chien and his friends cherished two young birds and carry them over. But after walking for a short distance, one bird is dead but his eyelids did not close, he must have missed his mother too much. Chien said to his teamamtes:

- As for this baby, I will try to take care of him!

- Can you guess what bird it is?

When he was a child, when he was herding buffaloes in the countryside, Ngoc was very passionate about raising birds, on the eaves of his house hung all kinds of bird cages: falcon, beaded, salute, green, red, etc. He can say immediately:

- The mouth is red, wide open like that, as far as I know, this is a Barracuda. It loves to eat chilies, really hot and spicy ones!

- Well, let's call it's Barracuda!... - Everyone agrees. From here, the bird was named "Barracuda", his future and career began to stick with "stranger friends" on every kilometer...

Listening to the whole "squad of people" eat while calculating food and water for a week on the peg, in the birdcage next to it, the Barracuda jumped on the food pipe, poked its head out the door to look at everyone, blinking its eyes. He blinked as if he was emotional when he heard people put himself on the list of those who would enjoy the precious few drops of water in that plastic can... It cried out a few times: if it's too complicated, let me go to the forest. Indeed, many times, Chien also felt sorry for him. He lives in a narrow cage, his wings were not exercised, his muscles seem to shrink more and more, and Chien wanted to release him back to the wild:

- The forest here is full of wild animals, is it safe if I let you out? Living on the peg with us is easy to get lost in bullets. Well, it's already "troublesome", you just keep going with us, I'll try to find some crickets and locusts for you, enough for a few days, okay? I won't let you starve or die of thirst. Ngoc said that you like to eat chili, your relatives must have met a lot of bitterness, right? - Chien feeds the bird while talking as if the bird understands. Being an animal, knowing how to eat, drink, and move, he also knows joy, sadness, anger and even love for the race!

After lunch on the way to the key position, the whole squad started to climb to the top of High Point 505. The sun burned everything. It rained heavily at night, but now this slope is dry. There was not a breeze, the trees around were quiet, drooping, and the climate was uncomfortable. The Pailin area is usually sunny in the morning and rainy in the afternoon. The dark clouds are racing to gather, gradually obscuring the forest patches to the west of the border, trying to prepare enough water for the rain this afternoon. Chien urged the squad to go quickly and get there in time before the storm hit. However, no matter how strong, no matter how much the squad leader urged, when halfway up the slope, everyone had to stop for a while to regain strength to continue. Suddenly, a series of machine guns fired from both sides. The whole squad fell into the enemy's ambush. Everyone quickly hid behind a tree, next to a rock to avoid bullets. Chien took advantage of a group of rocks like a frog's jaw, carrying the bird cage to get in. A plastic can of twenty liters of water that could not be brought along was left to dry in front of the cave. "I have to bring it in right away, or will get hit by bullets. The drop of water here is like a drop of blood, even more precious. If I get injured, I can still heal my skin, if the plastic can is punctured, where can I get water on this peg to use (!). Thinking so, Chien rushed out under the bullets, pulled the water can inside. Chien raised his head to observe along the slope from the top down. Seeing no one on the road, not even the enemy, he was relieved to think that his teammates had found a safe hiding place. The force holding on to the post was promptly mobilized to aid in the rescue.

- They shoot so bad! If the first bullet doesn't hit, it won't kill us! - A brother came out from a rock hole, dusted off his clothes, smiled with his white teeth, and spoke to the people from above. Not a single drop of water was lost, but one man was wounded, blood-soaked with bandages on his elbow.

- Our bird is still safe. After this, I'll reward you with locusts!

- What an unlucky day, Mr. Chien? - Ngoc asked the squad leader.

- Not that bad! We got into an ambush, both people and water are safe. One minor injury, not significant, the bird is still here. And meeting the enemy is natural. This is a front, not a resting place in My Khe beach or Son Tra peninsula. In my opinion, it's luck, not bad luck!... - Chien refutes Ho Ngoc's opinion.

The sun had already set the mountain far away when they reached the top. Standing on High Point 505 looking to the west, flocks of white storks flew back to perch on bamboo and coconut tops on the other side of the border. It's a peaceful place over there. The people over there have nothing to fear if they are not used in unnecessary trouble of the bloodthirsty people.

Chapter 7

The commander of the 2nd Battalion has yet to accept the ambiguous argument of the 1st Battalion politician at the Regiment Party Committee meeting last month. Buong thinks that Cat's stance could be more stable. The fight against the enemy to shed bones and blood on the front, from the point of view to action, must be clear and decisive, not inside or outside. Battalion commander Buong knew that Cat also disagreed with Secretary Binh. His double answer shows that he is struggling with something. Cat also understands, in order to keep the peg, he must bring his forces out, fight the enemy from afar, even have to block and attack them from the starting place, and must destroy them from their infancy. But why did he agree with Binh, that forces should not be sent out of the base, there must be some problem in the professional relationship, which led him to go in an unexpected direction. And if that is also Cat's point of view, then there is still no chance to prove it... That day, Buong also wanted to argue with Cat, argue with Cat is also argue with Binh, people have a saying: "Angry fish slashes. chop!", this guy seems to be also delicate. It appears that no one here wants to collide with the party secretary. Regiment Commander Manh is comfortable, when each issue is discussed, everyone is free to express their opinions. When no one else argued, he concluded. Sometimes, having completed, the regiment commander even asked: "Does anyone have any other ideas?". Therefore, after the end of an issue, it always creates a high consensus. Unlike the regiment commander, political commissar Truong Thanh Binh "blocked his throat" as soon as he discovered the views that he considered inappropriate. Buong was about to use the strategy of "shooting one arrow at two targets", but seeing regiment commander Xuan Manh stand up to conclude, he kept quiet, even though he was still unsettled in his heart.

When the 2nd battalion sent Chien's squad to the 505th post, the 1st battalion left Pailin town to build a defensive position to the north of the coffee plantation. Since Xuan Manh brought his regiment to this area, the 1st Battalion has always been beside the regimental headquarters. The 1st Battalion is a "baby", is a reserve force, always enjoys many privileges, and is not a "delicious food", but living near the regimental office in that crumbling neighborhood is a blessing. hundreds, thousands of times happier at the 505 peg, all day I see only dark clouds, the night is bone-chilling, the dry season is sunny and my skin burns, I always dream of having enough water to eat, drink, and bathe. Just thinking that, but here, no one is jealous, just follow the assignment of tasks, do not refuse, do not choose. Those in charge of the front, having the opportunity to go back, visit friends or spend the night in the 1st battalion all shared the same feeling: "It's a real baby, surrounded by units. The Pot soldiers who want to enter here must step "through the corpses" of the 2nd battalion in the west, the 3rd battalion in the east and how many "guys" are in the north (!)". The 1st Battalion still regularly maintains seven regimes during the day, during the week, morning exercise and afternoon sports while the wounded and sick soldiers are overloaded in the infirmary, most of them are soldiers of the 2nd battalion.

- We wish to live like you guys one day and die!...- There was a guy who was at High Point 505 who said it bluntly.

- Then you guys don't deserve all that we're getting... We need to live to fight. I'm also worried about what's going to happen next!

Now, the 1st Battalion went up to defend north of town, Cat expressed concern:

- Soldiers of the 2nd Battalion have been working hard for a long time. And we don't know what to do. In the town, sitting on the porch and falling asleep for a bit may be okay, now go up there be careful, Pot it sneaks in, stupidly it kills!...

Life is like that, so much happiness is so much suffering. Your "golden age" is over, now it's natural to have to pay the price! But I believe that you will quickly adapt to the living conditions in the new environment. Who doesn't! - According to Buong, those who live in a harsh environment must find every possible way to survive, never willing to sit and wait to die. Battalion 1 built a cluster of posts at the end of the coffee plantation. A company deployed at the crossroads of 10th and 58th streets. That morning, platoon leader Kiet sent a group to the forward post to meet the enemy from the north. The coffee plantation has been abandoned for a long time, the old trees are covered with grass, a few branches are still green, in season it still bears fruit. The smell of fragrant coffee flowers spreads, swarms of bee hover and scurry to collect honey. Soldier Nguyen Van Thanh was struggling to choose a position to work as a fortification on a mound, next to the coffee tree, he stepped on the left KP2 mine. The whole body of nearly 70kg collapsed like a banana tree being punished horizontally, fresh blood gushed out in puddles that dyed a piece of ground red, one leg was separated from the knee, the other leg was covered with a patch of skin. Thousands of miles have traveled from the Northeastern front to this extreme land for thousands of kilometers, through many villages, deep streams in pursuit of the fleeing enemy "with the flag". But now Thanh has to leave those feet under the red Pailin soil. Nguyen Van Thanh is a resident of a coastal city, a famous tourist destination of the Central region, he is preparing to return to the rear, but this hot land holds him back, because there are still teammates, so many fates are still struggling. struggling with the sun, rain, storms of harsh nature and this ruined town is threatened, in danger of falling into the hands of the enemy. Thanh volunteered to stay with his teammates in difficulty. "It's not like I'm turn away from you at this time (!)" - he thought, and today the misfortune happened.

Thanh has extraordinary energy, he does not groan but also asks his teammates: "Cut the other leg so that it won't get in my way!". Two transparent drops of water emerged from the corners of his eyes and then ran down his mouth, he fainted in the arms of his teammates... Waking up, looking down at his knees, "That's all!", Thanh shook his head and hid a sigh. The brothers had gathered all the bandages for the red knees, but they couldn't stop the blood still gushing out. They brought Thanh right to the surgery station, he was saved, but will have to stay in a wheelchair for the rest of his life. With a different desire to live, work, and surely the future of a Veteran, a wounded soldier "disabled but not disabled", Thanh will not sit idly by and let fate push him. Platoon leader Kiet had to send someone else to take Thanh's place. The compensation for the "relaxed" time enjoyed by the 1st Battalion began with the departure of those legs. Where Thanh "sticks" with a KP2 mine far from the main road, yesterday the platoon leader trampled this area, there is no place without his footprints. The rain at night has erased all traces. However, like here there are ghosts. Surely they are still around somewhere.

- The regimental commander saw the danger from base 321 directly threatening the town of Pailin in the north, so he sent the 1st battalion there. This has "reinforced" the point of view of Secretary Binh that it is necessary to increase the level of solidity for the fortifications rather than carrying troops to place them here, throwing them there, to avoid casualties. And of course, no one in the 1st Battalion wanted to leave the place near the regimental headquarters to go up there…

Chapter 8

The Chief of the General, Ta Mok, urged his subordinates to build a solid 321 base. He agreed with Minister of Foreign Affairs, Ieng Sary, that it would not be easy to regain Pailin. In the valley, although the enemy had only one regiment, there were many other forces surrounding it. They were not foolish enough to be isolated. Bypassing the outer ring, breaking in and fighting from the inside out, as they often called "blooming in the enemy's heart,"? Even if they were able to control this town, the enemy would not simply sit still and let them do as they pleased. If they used the strategy of "attacking the point and destroying the reinforcement" they would lack the necessary power and human resources to attack the town or block reinforcements from outside. Ta Mok had already secured the high ground at 321, so he knew he needed to establish a firm foothold and turn it into a springboard to stop enemy reinforcements from the North. When the opportunity arose, they could strike directly at Pailin. Alternatively, he would devise his own strategy. He nodded in agreement with his own plan and began silently preparing to deploy troops and arrange the battle in a "reciprocal, next-generation" way.

-I agree with the Minister's opinion! - He lifted his eyes to encourage Xa Ry. Standing here serves two purposes: to attack and prevent, to block and to attack. If 321 is attacked, this will be their burial ground, "when the buffalo dies, the cow is skinned too"... We will strengthen the besieging forces, isolate Pailin until there is a chance!

The exiled reactionary government was anxiously awaiting a solution to the Cambodia problem. Preparations and construction of the battle were carried out quietly with great urgency. Ta Mok's headquarters were located on the southern slopes of the mountain, offering an excellent view of Pailin town. However, the element of surprise had been lost after an incident where three girls encountered a stranger while bathing at the source of the Sank Ke river. The girls had been unable to grab their clothes and had fled back to the base naked. They were terrified and out of breath when reporting the incident. Upon hearing their story, a group of black-uniformed soldiers was dispatched to examine the situation.

"It is true that the 'Duon' has reached behind us! Here, they left this!" the leader of the black-shirted team said, picking up a bag of dried rice labeled 'made in Vietnam' from a noodle factory in Saigon and bringing it to the senior. The bag of dried rice had been accidentally left behind by a soldier in Chien's squad when the whole squad took turns watching the girls bathing in the stream. In response, a group of soldiers in black clothes carried mines and scattered them in the area, then fired mortars from afar.

At 505 base, Tran Duy Chien raised binoculars to observe. Each convoy of rudimentary vehicles and heavy-lifted pedestrians, from the southern forest, rushed to the north. Ta Mok was mobilizing forces to transport weapons, ammunition and equipment to the area opposite the 321 ridge across the border to implement the crazy idea of building a springboard here. Newly transported mines and ammunition boxes from the Co Cong mountains, still smelling of turpentine, whole belts, and raw materials were piled up along the border. The units that were said to be "good at fighting" Ta Mok had deployed here, stretching from Com Rieng to the south for kilometers like "disguised refugee camps" so far along the Cambodia-Thailand border. A secret road was opened from the West to 321 ridge. Ta Mok sent an "old soldier platoon", a notoriously evil soldier to manage that road. He ordered:

-Whoever up there retreats, shoot! - He pointed to the high point in front of him. Must stick to the end!...

Around the hillside, mines were planted in layers: pedal mines, entangled mines, high jump mines, low jump mines, mines hanging from trees, mines buried in the ground, next to the tree, next to the termite mound... Only one exit was left, and it seemed that even the mouse could not get through. The 321 ridge was full of rocks, the black rock blocks like a buffalo leaning against each other, no need to do any fortifications, thoroughly taking advantage of the terrain to fight. What is building fortifications for, the enemy coming up here will expose themselves on the ground. Ta Mok was truly a man with battle experience. He rose to the top of his power thanks to his killing experience on the battlefield, like a wild beast, the more soldiers he died, the higher he climbed.

The Pailin Valley resembled a chessboard, with pieces from both sides moving in their final moves. More and more enemy groups began to appear around the 1st Infantry Battalion. Standing at the crossroads of 10th and 58th streets, looking to the North in sight, people sometimes see soldiers in black clothes crossing the road and disappearing in the coffee garden interspersed with weeds. A flock of parrots with light blue feathers, chirping on the peach trees, jumped up in surprise, then tilted their wings and flew to the East, not daring to turn back. 120 mm mortars rained down from the border day and night, causing the trench fortifications of the 1st Battalion soldiers to collapse.

The rainy season had passed, the dry season officially arrived in the Pailin mountains. In the morning, the air was cold, but in the afternoon and afternoon the sun was bright, like burning. Thanks to the enemy's bullets, just a few days after coming here, the 1st Battalion's battlefield had become more solid than ever. Between life and death, everyone takes care of themselves with an "armor" to keep their head. Like in the old days, the war with the Americans, those who stayed in the forest forever, when they came down to the plains, they often felt empty, had a cold back, exposed plank. If they wanted to live with the helicopters, it took a while, sometimes at the cost of human lives. After Nguyen Van Thanh lost his legs and the sudden deaths of many people, the 1st Battalion also gradually adapted to the living conditions in the new place. All soldiers' activities were carried out in the trenches, in sturdy bunkers. Because of that, they huddled together like hedgehogs in a cave.

One morning, just waking up at dawn, the roosters were calling each other under the bamboo row on the bank of the ford, the guards around the 1st battalion reported at the same time: an enemy appeared in close range. Battalion commander Khang alerted the fighting position. Lam took a gun and ran out, as soon as he stepped into the battle pit, he stepped on the landmine and jumped, collapsed on the edge of the trench, his intestines and lungs were scattered everywhere, blood flowed out, seeping into the ground. From the North and the Northwest, bullets from medium-machine guns, heavy-machine-gun, B40, B41 ... were thick in front of the battlefield. The 60 and 82mm mortars exploded all around. Thanks to the strong fortification, there was no major damage, except for Lam "deaf" who died and three people were injured. The artillery barrage of the regiment intervened in time and muzzled some of their mortars. Battalion commander Khang immediately dispatched a platoon to break through the bullets and attack the flanks. Soldier Tho just jumped over the trench, stepped on the right mine, fell down and died on the spot with two seriously injured people. On the north side, the 3rd company also had a similar situation. The enemy could not break into our battlefield, but the 1st Battalion suffered too much pain... The regimental infirmary was overloaded, and now it was "added" new cases.

When staying in 505 ridge, Chien's squad was shocked when they heard that two comrades had died. Among the sacrifices, Chien had a close friend from the same hometown who joined the army on the same day, that was Lam "deaf".

- Lam! So you're ahead of me! We made a promise that whoever was still alive had to bring the other's remains back. Now I don't know if I'm still alive to bring you back to the motherland. When I heard that you passed away, I was like a person who lost his soul and was panic-stricken. There are no conditions here to burn incense for you!... I can only visit your soul with a few poems!... - Chien moved his mouth as if whispering to his friend and took out the notebook to write: *This noon / The forest bird does not sing / Sad clouds embrace the mountains / The news that you decreased hastily returned to the peg / I was dumbfounded like a lost soul / Brother! Comrades! / Tears are shed to mourn for you...*

As Chien's squad mourned, tears streamed down everyone's faces. Chien entered the cellar, his hands trembling, and retrieved a bowl of rice. With solemn reverence, he placed it at the center of the hill where Tho and Lam had fallen that morning. The five brothers knelt together, united in their grief.

"We will bring your remains back to your hometown," they vowed. "One of us will live to fulfill this promise!"

In the vast darkness, the sunset cast long shadows that swallowed the hill and its inhabitants, as if effortlessly ending the fates of these volunteer soldiers on the international battlefield...

Chapter 9

Chien's squad received two messages on the same day. At noon, they heard the heartbreaking news of Tho and Lam's sacrifice, and at 9 o'clock at night, the battalion informed them via a two-way phone call to attend the congress. Devastated by the loss of their comrades, all five brothers cried until they ran out of tears. Later that night, when Chien received the news about the congress, he was unsure whether to be happy or sad.

- "Chien, prepare to leave tomorrow morning!" ordered the leader. "Go down and buy us some things, mainly cigarettes and writing paper!" Seeing that Chien hesitated, his brothers reminded him. Everyone was happy for him and hoped that after the trip, there would be cigarettes, writing papers, and their simple requests would be met. Chien refuse categorically:

- "No, I'm not going anywhere, I'll stay here with you guys. I have no merit to join the 'celebration'!

- "Come on, Chien, just go for a few days. You can smoke freely and won't have to dig around for 'samples' like you did today. We'll take care of things here for you. Those who still have money can give it to you to buy things. The other day, I picked up several dozen stones. You can take them and exchange them for a few packs of filter cigarettes to smoke up here. Also, you can go to some 'uncles' at the gold shop and tell them it is Pailin red stone, and they will take them all. The Sophia stone is used for inlaying rings and making jewelry for women, or for attaching to watches, which looks very beautiful!..."

Ngoc ran into the cellar, rummaged through his backpack, took out dozens of stone beads to put in the palm of his hand, the sunlight shining in showed the iridescent color of blue, red, purple, yellow. Each stone was only half the size of a grain of rice. In the town of Pailin, after rain, the rays of light shined on the pavement or the courtyards have peeled off the tiles, standing on the balconies of the houses looking down to see iridescent like morning dew drops. Although the value of the stones was not much, there have been a number of officers and soldiers here who have been disciplined, many times in meetings, political commissar Binh mentioned it as the content of the monthly review.

Despite his reluctance to attend the "Celebration Congress," Captain Tran Duy Chien felt a deep responsibility to represent his platoon and battalion. He wanted to learn from the combat experiences of others and seek revenge for his fallen comrades. Standing at the entrance to the bunker of 505 check point where he had spent countless nights enduring harsh weather, mosquito bites, and bone-chilling cold, he gazed at everything around him with a sense of familiarity and longing. The kerosene lamp hung on the wall, the water bucket, the backpack shelf, the hammock pole, and even the toothbrush stuck in a bottle were all too familiar and dear to him.

The moment reminded him of the time he had left his old, dilapidated house in Da Nang to embark on a mission. Suddenly, two tears rolled down his cheeks, stinging his nose. Chien lit a cigarette and sat down to record his diary, something he had been doing regularly since arriving at 505. He wrote more concisely now because his notebook was almost full. He imagined what would happen at the "Celebration Congress" and what he would say if asked to give a speech, what his manner and clothes would be, how he would answer the chief officer. This time he would most likely meet "Thinh Wrinkle," the battalion commander at the training school who always had a wrinkled face. Despite his appearance, Thinh was a kind-hearted person who cared deeply about his soldiers. During his time as a teacher at the Officer Candidate School, he acted as a fatherly figure to his young soldiers. Due to his many wrinkles, he earned the nickname "Thinh Wrinkle." Chien was excited to see him again. At the moment he was planning his next steps after leaving 505 and arriving in the town of Pailin to join the division: first he needed to get a haircut, wash his clothes, take a bath, and visit his friends. At night, after writing in his diary, he would sleep to make up for the stressful week he had endured. When he returned to the division office, his first priority would be to visit the graves of his fallen comrades at the airport cemetery. During the days of the Congress, he and his fellow soldiers took the opportunity to buy things their comrades had sent, including writing paper, notebooks, pens, and cigarettes.

Chien sat motionless, his eyes fixed on a distant and indefinite point in the flickering kerosene lamp light.

The night at the border was tranquil, punctuated by the pleasant blend of two seasons. From within the warm bunker, the melodic chirping of crickets and the sonorous croaks of frogs in the distant trees could be heard. The moon had disappeared, leaving the deep, starry sky above. Chien leaned back into the hammock that was already hung in the corner of the bunker, the oil lamp flickering and casting half of the hammock like a small boat navigating through the vast ocean in the rainy season. Suddenly, a mortar shell exploded nearby, causing the bunker roof to shake and the stones on the wall to tremble and fall, waking Chien up. Hastily grabbing his gun, he exited the bunker, only to be swallowed by the engulfing darkness that surrounded 505. All was calm, Ngoc's shadow remained vigilant under the tree. Chien returned to his hammock, but his thoughts were consumed with the memory of his fallen friends from the previous day. He tried to clear his mind by counting to two thousand, but found no respite. Sometimes, he shifted positions on the hammock, causing the bird in the bamboo cage to become restless. In a moment of compassion, he remembered his Hill Myna, whom he suspected hadn't eaten anything that evening. He got up and headed to Hill Myna's place, reassuring and comforting him.

"The light is dim now, and I can't see the way. Tomorrow, I'll bring you something to eat. The rice is still there, and it will be even tastier when you're hungry. I'll be away for a few days, but those who remain here are my closest friends and teammates. They're good people, and if you need anything, just call out!"

The bird seemed to understand, jumping a few times before lying still. Chien returned to his hammock and remembered that he had two cigarettes left in his pocket. He sat up, retrieved a lighter from his shirt, and lit a cigarette, inhaling deeply and holding the smoke in his lungs. The smoke permeated every cell in his body, causing his limbs to tremble and his movements to be unsteady. Chien leaned against a post and lay back down on the hammock, feeling the bunker spin and the world turn. Then, before knowing it, he had already fallen asleep.

Chapter 10

This morning, Platoon leader Kiet led a group to the front post, which the soldiers called the "shrimp antenna". Hiding in a coffee lot overgrown with plants, a soldier asked:

-Why is it not called "the crossroad of road 10" here for the right terrain, but called "the crossroad in red soil" Mr. Kiet?!

-This crossroad is not on the 10 street, it is about 100 meters north and about the same west of the road 58. As for "red soil", do you understand? You guys need to remember, this is the peg with the nature of covert operation, lying there to catch the enemy's muzzle poked into the left flank of the battalion. These guys often sneak up to strike at our vulnerabilities! - Kiet carefully explained to his soldiers about the enemy's plots and tricks and the purpose of bringing the team here before the enemy could break in. Kiet took the lead, behind were Son and two soldiers. The bright sunlight covered the Pailin valley, the hot wind passed his face, and the scorching heat burnt the skin. The old coffee trees had shed all their leaves. The dried coffee leaves crackled like roasted rice crackers when touched together. Just a single cigarette butt falling on them could ignite and burn down the entire forest in an instant. The dusty bazan soil was blown up into a haze, obscuring the paths. The winding streams embraced the town, once full of water last month, now left only rocks and sand. The soldiers here were easy to distinguish from those in other areas, as they always carried a bamboo tube full of water behind their backs. The water from the bottle flowed into the body and seeped out through the pores, soaking the clothes before dispersing into the air. During the dry season, the need for water was always a top priority for the soldiers. If anyone didn't want to collapse on the road, they had to take care of their own water supply. No one told anyone else what to do, and there was no need for a party resolution or waiting for orders from the commander. Each person had to find their own bamboo tube, and the platoon and company had as many bamboo tubes as they had people. Each bamboo tube was a long tube of four to five spans. If all the bamboo tubes of the entire battalion were connected, it would stretch for miles...No one in the battalion 3 forgot the disaster caused by a lack of water during the dry season last year at the Cao Me Lai mountain forest, when they and the first battalion attacked the Central Office of the Three Factions. While other people were celebrating the achievement of their goal, they had to carry each other back because of the lack of water. Lips cracked, soldiers collapsed in the khooc forest, under the dry rocky stream beds...Everyone in Son's unit carried water, walking together with the sound of sloshing. Four people jumped onto the edge of the trench and across the gap to the other side when gunfire erupted from the right side, followed by B40-41 shells and grenades exploding around them.

-Lay down! - Platoon commander Kiet shouted when the whole unit fell into the enemy's ambush in the gap between two broken trenches.

The 82mm mortar battle of the Battalion 1 responded in time, saving "a loose" for his teammates. Thanks to that, leader Kiet was able to overcome the enemy's ambush without anyone getting injured or bleeded, but the spirit of some was shaken...

Leader Son threw himself into the trench, feeling that his right calf was wet and cold, he bent down to see. One leg of his pants was soaked, and Son raised his hand to lift the bottom of the convex aluminum ball, which was empty and light. As it turned out, a bullet made the bottle with nearly a liter of water punctured a large hole, enough to fit a thumb; water came out and there was not a drop left.

-Hehe. I am so lucky. If the bottle did not "catch the bullet", I would lose a leg!

Kính walked beside Son and asked:

-Does it take long to stay here, Mr. Son?

-When someone comes out here instead, we will know!

-Then why should I even ask you! - Kinh raised his voice to the leader.

Since the day Son's unit came here, the road behind had worn out: the fellow soldier carried food up, weapons down to supplement ammunition, kept communication with the platoon to deliver letters to the checkpoints..., all have to go through here. The gap between the two battle zones, where the enemy launched an ambush yesterday, has also been connected, all movements up and down are carried out under the battle zone, but Kinh is still afraid...

For more than ten days now, the soldiers had gone without a proper bath. The scarce rainfall provided little water for drinking, let alone washing. To overcome this, he had dug a square hole under the battle zone, measuring about one meter wide and thirty centimeters deep. He had laid a green nylon sheet at the bottom of the hole, and the rear forces had brought water up to fill it as a reserve, to provide water for the entire platoon for eating and drinking. The unit leader had been keeping a close eye on the water hole, even sleeping next to it. But last night, someone had sneaked in and stolen some water. This morning, Kinh passed by and saw no one around, so he dipped a dark yellow, Bazan dirt-colored handkerchief stiff like a mud scoop, dipped it into the water hole, and squeezed the water from the handkerchief into the bottle, but he was caught "red-handed" by the team leader when he returned from the restroom

-So these days you stole water from the group. I will report to the platoon leader!

-No! I just came out today. I was on the peg all week. You mistakenly blame me for that!

- We has been losing water these days, if it was not you then who?!

-I don't know! - Saying that, Kinh went to the front. The leader of the army rearing unit was about to force Kinh to return the water bottle, but he thought: "they are also working hard (!)" - so he let him go. The harsh climate, cold nights and hot days, living under the battle trenches without being able to bathe, scabies began to attack. In the armpits and groin, everyone had inflammation, ulcers when walking and standing, legs had to be spread wide like a compass. The platoon's budget struggled to follow the party cell resolution of "one hot, two cold", but many days they had to use "three colds" too. Eating dry rice with salt, their diet was dry and many people suffered from edema and constipation.

"Last time I heard you say you were peeing blood, is it better now? You look chubby!" Seeing Kinh's tight skin and his eyes half-closed like a sleep-deprived person, Son sympathetically asked.

"Staying here and eating this little will not make you fat, three bites of rice are only enough to sustain life... it might be edema. Nurse comes to have some vitamin B1, Son"

"Drinking vitamin B1 will make you very hungry very soon, where will you get food to eat?" Son also felt like his face was a bit swollen. He bent down, pressed his index finger on the ankle bone, his skin sagged for a moment before filling back up.

The leader of the platoon 1 believed that in order to maintain this budget checkpoint, they must first secure the path from the back to the front, and deploy forces to sweep from a distance. The entire battalion was expanding its range of operations. For over a week, Son's team had not been relieved, and the three of them were still in the "leg-bench" position. Leader Kiet declared:

"From now on, whoever loses someone has to make up for it!

It had been almost a week, but the platoon hadn't received any mail, and the ammunition hadn't been replenished. The old newspapers were being passed around among the unit, with everyone reading every word and tearing off a piece to roll into cigarettes to satisfy their cravings. During lunchtime, Kinh found some dried leaves in the deserted garden next to a red dirt slope. He took the leaves back to the bunker, cut them into pieces, then rolled them into a makeshift joint and lit it up. After inhaling a few puffs, he stood up and began to stagger and sway, finally collapsing onto the ground and laughing uncontrollably, until he began to cry. He kept laughing and then crying, then laughing,... The platoon leader, Son, became furious, "If you're laughing like that, you're giving away our position, what are you doing?"

"Shut up!" Son slapped him half-heartedly, but Kinh kept laughing.

Hearing the commotion, the squad leader, Kiet, came to check, only to find Kinh smoking marijuana. He explained:

"Marijuana is a type of drug that can be addictive. When you don't have it, you can't bear it. In Cambodia, they use it to feed pigs. When they put marijuana leaves in the pig's feed, the pig will sleep all day without running around, saving energy and gaining weight quickly. You guys didn't know, marijuana is illegal. Like poppy plants, if you plant or store them, you will go to jail!"

- Oh, I see. We didn't know!

From then on, whenever they craved it, some of the soldiers would look for marijuana leaves to smoke, leaving them dazed and disoriented. Some even sent marijuana leaves home for their wives to feed their pigs.

The next morning at around 5 o'clock, Son's platoon encountered an incident. When they couldn't see the enemy's face, the sound of gunfire echoed through the silent night, and the mist settled over the paths. It was Kinh's turn to stand guard that night. Every night, Son usually took charge of the guard duty during the busiest hours. But he noticed that Kinh wasn't feeling well lately, so he gave him the last shift, which ended at 5 o'clock. At that time, all activities in this checkpoint had already started. Son handed over the position to Kinh and then retreated to a nearby trench with a hammock inside. The warmth of Kinh's body remained, causing Son to fall asleep almost instantly. After a while, he woke up with a start at the sound of a gunshot echoing in the distance. The platoon leader quickly got up, left the hammock, grabbed his AK, and ran out of the trench.

The wind blew through the mountains, and the leaves playfully rustled and whispered on the edge of the battlefield. The sickle moon was high in the sky, casting a silver glow over the deserted and cold battlefield. The buzzing of insects never ceased. From the money checkpoint, Kinh put his gun over his shoulder, his right hand tightly holding his left arm, and ran towards the trench. Without paying attention, he collided with Son, who was also running towards him from behind, and both almost fell over.

- I'm injured, Son! - he said as he took off his gun and leaned against the edge of the trench. His right hand still held the bleeding wound, wetting the sleeve of his shirt.

- What happened, Kinh? - Son asked, concerned.

- Two enemies attacked me. I just aimed and fired, but their guns went off first and injured me. Oh, it hurts so much. Please bandage it for me!

- Did you manage to fire any shots? Son asked as he examined the wound. Kinh was embarrassed.

- No. But I think I fired a few shots!

Hearing the sound of gunfire, Minh number 2 in the nearby bunker rushed to provide support.

- Comrade, take your position and watch out for the enemy. I'll bandage Kinh's wound and come right back! - Son urged Minh.

The platoon leader Son felt that something was a bit illogical in this situation. If the enemy was launching an attack, they would usually fire more than just a few shots, not only with AK but also with B40 and B41. There should be the sound of bullets whizzing through the air, unless the bullets were embedded in the ground. When bandaging Kinh's wound, Son saw that the bullet went through his arm, and a piece of flesh was blown away by the bullet. Son even had a feeling that when they first met, he handed the gun to Kinh, and the barrel was still hot, indicating that Kinh had fired the gun. A thought crossed his mind: "He caused this to himself (!)." He thought so, but he did not tell anyone, as they were still in combat and he did not want to affect the unit. Kinh was transferred to the rear. Platoon leader Kiet replaced Kinh with another soldier.

Then, for many nights, Son laid on the hammock, unable to sleep, and wondered whether he should report his suspicions about Kinh's injury. Kinh was his friend from their hometown, and they had many memories together under the bamboo trees. Should he speak out and "betray" him? Now revealing everything is like exposing the back of the garment to the public. However, I can sense it even in silence. Everyone here is the same, far from home, enduring rain and sunshine, living and dying together. Then Sơn thinks back to the early days, putting on a backpack and coming here, enduring fever, thirst, hunger, and wearing tattered clothes, missing home, missing the homeland until it hurts to the core, and witnessing many terrible deaths of comrades in this devastated town so that today, the history of a heroic unit is supplemented with glorious pages. There was a time when Sơn was also shaken, intending to find some reason to escape from this godforsaken place. However, Sơn never had the courage to do it, even to think about something so "shocking" like Kính did today - shooting himself in the hand to return to the rear. No, Sơn would never do that. Doing so is cowardice, surrendering in battle, and surrendering to the enemy. If you have the courage to shoot yourself, why not stand there and shoot the enemy? If you die or get injured, your homeland and family will be proud to have a son sacrificed for the country. The more he thought, the more regretful Sơn felt, regretting the thoughtless actions of his friend. It was no wonder that since coming to this spending checkpoint, Sơn had seen him seem depressed, with a sad face. Presumably, over the past few days, he struggled in his heart. Well, the incident had happened, just consider it a regrettable incident in his life! ... Life is long, and there are still many opportunities for those who run away. Sơn thought that Kính didn't have to suffer like him, struggling; he was the youngest, being pampered by his parents, given full education, not having to toil like others. He had to quit college to join the army and couldn't endure the hardships. His action was not a betrayal, but a way to escape from suffering, to find pleasure and material needs. Thinking that, Sơn felt satisfied with himself that he overcame all the difficulties and obstacles on this front from the beginning until now.

The weather had changed seasons, the remaining dark clouds gradually dissipated in the bright sunshine. The sky was wide open, deep blue. "The crossroad in red soil" was nestled in the Pailin valley, blurred in the pale pink dust of basaltic soil. The front line was quiet that day. Chief Le Thanh Son felt peaceful deep down.

Kính was transferred to the hospital on the rear. In his medical records, there was a strong question mark. Perhaps this incident had not stopped there...

Chapter 11

While Nguyen Mong Hung was talking about the battalion commanded by Captain Ngo Xuan Manh, both Chi Tai and Phearak listened attentively, not missing any details. Phearak, in particular, seemed proud of his father who had fought fiercely on the very land where he was born - a seed sown and nurtured from an unexpected love between a volunteer soldier and his mother, a flower that bloomed amidst the ruins. These expressions only fueled Mong Hung's passion for the story, and he continued on:

Scout platoon leader Mai led a team to investigate base 321 at the Parrot Beak area. "Hung Black" brought a calculator to study the frontal direction, which the Hung Battalion was responsible for. Identifying this combat target on this front is difficult, but it must be done. People often say, "know the enemy, know yourself, and you will win a hundred battles." Sometimes, even if you know the enemy, you still fail in battle. If you don't know anything about them, how can you avoid failure?

Ngo Xuan Manh, the battalion leader, still remembered that when he set foot on this front line, enemies surrounded him on all sides. When he went down to the stream to fetch water, he saw a few black-clad guerrillas passing by like ghosts, disappearing into the coffee garden. When he reached the stream bank, he stepped on a mine. There were mines everywhere in the town's ruined area, along the roadsides, under the trees, beside the latrines... As Tran Duy Chien wrote in his diary: *"Every step we take is rough and rugged/ Mines explode with a thunderous roar, flesh and bones fly..."*

The volunteer soldiers on the front knew the enemy only through their tactics of landmines, ambushes, raids, and silent shootings. They didn't bother themselves with which division the target belonged to or which section of the road was under which battalion's responsibility. However, Battalion Chief Xuan Manh knew that the more difficult the target, the more thorough the knowledge needed. This was a difficult task, as nobody had been able to determine how many divisions existed on the northwestern front, their identities, or even their commanders. The border bases still existed openly, and the reconnaissance rarely penetrated their defenses to infiltrate their bases. This was partly due to the army's lack of experience and not having adapted to new combat methods on a new battlefield. At the same time, on the front line, it was evident that Ta Mok was sly and no one knew what his intentions were. During the conquest of the Cao Me Lai base, it was thought there would be fierce resistance, but there were only a few rough works, makeshift camps, and warehouses that were almost worthless except for a few guns and bullets. If equipped for a regular battalion, it would still need many supplements. Despite this, bases like this continued to exist for decades to come. They grew like weeds on the battlefield, uprooted one, and another one sprouted up. Erase bases on the border and they would appear inland. They crawled into Phum, Sok and climbed up in the revolutionary government as "two-faced, double crosser" elements. It was strange that at the United Nations General Assembly, there were "two people sitting." Ta Mok was so unpredictable that no book was written about him. He acted according to a pattern of "no pattern at all." In terms of cruelty, nobody in the 20th century could surpass him except for Hitler. By the time, he was concerned about adding more crimes against humanity…

To conduct a thorough investigation of the combatants, Battalion Commander Xuan Manh deployed experienced scouts to search the valley, identify targets, and verify the identity of each specific target to apply appropriate tactics. One of the platoons headed south and came across three girls bathing under a waterfall. Although suspected to be Thai people who came to exploit forest products, there could be a unit of Khmer Rouge soldiers in the area. It was necessary to investigate which division they belonged to: 221, 415, or 162. Another team was sent to investigate base 321 in detail, and it was identified as belonging to the 415th special forces. The soldiers only needed to study its backside to launch a surprise attack when necessary.

On the front line of the battalion, the commander assigned independent combat operations to the first platoon of the Hung "black" unit. Mai's unit departed at 3:30 pm, a time when the enemy usually regrouped to return to their base after a day of harassing their forward positions. They headed northward through the forest towards the "Parrot Beak" area. The Pailin region had entered the rainy season, and the trees were waiting for the water under the scorching tropical sun. After the rain, the trees bloomed with smiles, and bees and butterflies buzzed, calling for mates and seeking nectar. The streams snaked through the dilapidated streets, now containing muddy pools that could provide enough water for each soldier to fill a large water bottle and hang it on their waist.

After filling up the bottle, Platoon Leader Mai ordered them to move forward to reach the target before dusk. The forest there was dense with intertwined thorny bamboo thickets, and some places required crawling like a lizard to get through. They also had to worry about mines buried under the ground or hanging on the trees. At night, even the most skilled could not move more than a few dozen meters, let alone the scout team that had to overcome obstacles of over 500 meters. Mai calculated the time so that they would arrive at the border line after crossing the minefield when it was just getting dark.

Boss Tà Mok ordered his troops to lay mines along the border and 321 ridge. The areas where the mines were placed were carefully selected to ensure maximum surprise, with no troops operating in those areas. The soldiers' ability was the main weakness, which was why he chose two highly skilled soldiers in enemy mine detection techniques. They would navigate through the obstacle field, moving straight west and not avoiding difficult areas. Despite crawling and climbing over sharp thorns and dense trees, they would remove the mines to create a path for their unit. The fewer soldiers and lighter the equipment, the better. These reconnaissance soldiers were trained to understand the risks and accept losses if necessary, crawling back to their unit at all costs without being carried.... They were not afraid of being lost, simply because they were reconnaissance soldiers. They could detect any sign of strangers, such as a bird suddenly flying away or insects becoming quiet at night - the insects really had heightened senses. By looking at a tree, they could determine the four and eight directions. Only when they close their eyes and stop breathing could they be considered lost.

Since the previous day, the first few raindrops sprinkled down did not reduce the heat, but on the contrary, the air became more and more sultry and stuffy. It seemed that the humidity was just enough for the mosquito swarm to multiply, multiply exponentially, and increase rapidly. Mosquitoes were like rice husks, everywhere you touch them, you would see round mosquitoes, your hand would hit your butt, your cheek would feel wet, and you would see a fishy smell of blood on your nose and want to vomit. You guys are free to bite, but there's nothing to do with each other, here people who only wear shorts, smear the pot black, and don't dare to hit those mosquitoes with their hands, if they hit the mosquitoes their opponent would smash back. This was the time to suck blood for hungry mosquitoes. Several times Mai had to remind the soldiers that they were close to the enemy, had to keep it a secret, if the mosquito bite was too itchy, just rub it. The group of three formed a vertical line like an arrow through a minefield. Occasionally, the foot accidentally stepped on the dry branches and they heard the crackling sound. Wherever they went, the insects groaned silently.

After midnight, when the high moon rises, spreading a layer of silver light on the green forest carpet, making the night dew drops like pearls, the 321 ridge appeared behind. Mai paused for a moment to determine the direction. The scout unit kept groping, straining their eyes to see through the dim night. A trail appeared in front of them, coming from the south and turning east towards the foot of peak 321. Mai signaled to the two soldiers behind him. The three of them hid in the bushes and thickets, their eyes fixed on both ends of the road, listening intently with their ears close to the ground to detect any sound. The sound of heavy footsteps grew louder from afar, and then a group of people emerged. One of them stopped by the roadside, unzipped his pants, and relieved himself. A warm stream of urine poured down on Mai's head... "What did you drink that makes your pee smell so bad?" Mai thought to himself. The man finished and hurriedly caught up with his comrades. Mai breathed a sigh of relief. He whispered to the two soldiers next to him

\- We can ambush them here!

But then Mai wondered, where was their target? Where was their base?... Tà Mok! What kind of trick are you playing, Tà Mok? Where are your soldiers? Mai was disappointed that he had not found any specific target. "Or maybe we should just wait here and see if any of them go alone, capture one and interrogate them (!)". This bold idea was not new to Mai. When he was in school, he remembered the most effective reconnaissance method was to "capture prisoners of war." During the war against America, there was a time when Mai commanded a reconnaissance team to approach a target through an abandoned village in the 5th district battlefield. That night, like tonight, Mai crawled into a pit in the corner of a garden to check, but a guerrilla soldier crawled out from under the pit. Their faces met. Without thinking, Mai pointed his gun at the soldier's nose and whispered, "Raise your hands, resist me and I'll shoot you!..." The guerrilla soldier shook with fear, his mouth shut, unable to make a sound, obediently raising his hands above his head. Mai asked, "Is there anyone else in the pit?" The soldier shook his head. Mai ordered:

\- Follow me, and I will spare you!

So Mai took him and brought him to a place for asking:

-Are there many soldiers in the garrison?

-There are very few people inside. Most of them have already gone outside and laid down!

If we hadn't caught that soldier that day, our army would have attacked the empty land... Now, here in Pol Pot, the soldiers were also human beings, mostly people, except for some stubborn people in the central area and those who owed a lot of blood to the people, they were also humans but acted like animals, they were very stubborn. But soldiers may have to hold guns because of this situation or that reason, if they are enlightened, fed, and spoken to, they will confess everything. Who doesn't want to live, afraid of death. But then Mai thought of the way back. From here to Pailin is too difficult, too dangerous. If we catch the prisoner, can we bring him back? We don't know the Cambodian language to interrogate him on the spot.

While Mai was thinking, suddenly there was a woman's voice and then flames flickered at the foot of the mountain. Mai reached out his arm to where there was a faint light in the night sky, looking at his watch. "Oh no, it's almost four thirty in the morning (!)". Concentrating on observing the enemy, Mai forgot about time. Perhaps the signs that had just appeared were the enemy's base at the foot of the mountain, to the West at 321 ridge. Have they started cooking breakfast yet? We must go back immediately, if we are late we will not be able to cross the border...

The afternoon rain had made the air on the border region chilly this morning, the cold was pleasant. After a sleepless night, the reconnaissance soldiers were still alert, touching their skin, feeling smooth and soft because of the mixture of pot dirt and wild vegetable leaves that were applied since last night. To the East, the dawn had broken, the wild chickens were crowing to each other in the battlefield. Everything in this border region was awakened, coming alive after a dark night, tired from the changing weather. The reconnaissance platoon commanded by Captain Mai was returning to the "land of ours" at the Parrot Beak area.

Suddenly, from behind, a volley of continuous gunfire sounded, B40 bullets flying forward and backward. Several tree branches were hit and fell down, the ground and rocks were flying, the smell of gunpowder choking in the mouth, the nose, the eyes stinging without a way out...

In the morning, the night dew lingered on the leaves, the grass, the reconnaissance team did not have time to erase their traces, a border patrol unit discovered and unexpectedly attacked from behind. Captain Mai fell down immediately from the first barrage. Two soldiers were bewildered, not knowing where the enemy was, when a soldier in ragged clothes shouted and rushed towards them....

The scout leader hurriedly took his bag to the command post:

-Report to the regimental commander, in the northwest direction, the reconnaissance team on the way back to the Parrot's Beak, was ambushed by the enemy, comrade Mai died, two soldiers escaped!... A group of the 1st battalion left capturing the enemy in the west at peg 505 also met the enemy and opened fire. Comrade Hung may have lost his way!...

Xuan Manh was stunned by the unexpected news. There were many reasons for his concern: Mai was an experienced scout. He has enough courage to take on higher positions. The position of captain was too much for him. But... And Hung "black" was a promising officer. The position of chief of staff was waiting for him. All the plans of the regiment in the past on this Pailin front marked the significant contribution of Hung "black". The regimental commander had great confidence in his subordinate commander. Over the years, standing shoulder to shoulder on the battlefield, Manh did not worry at all about the loyalty of a party member, a battalion cadre like "Hung Den", a humorous name that has become affectionate, familiar to all officers and soldiers in the regiment that always stood at the most dangerous position. But against the enemy's malicious schemes and tricks, will he be able to keep his sense of purpose and uprightness when he accidentally falls into the enemy's hands...

The three people, Regiment Commander Xuan Manh, Chief of Staff Thanh and the Chief of Reconnaissance, sat at the table, their heads together, and focused their eyes on the map of the Pailin area.

-According to the report of two scout soldiers who went with Mr. Mai to run back, the brothers managed to slip through the back of base 321. Across the border there is a trail from the South up to turn to the 321 ridge. This could be the supply line up from the direction of Co Cong or from a nearby logistics base supplying 321! - The scout leader commented.

The Chief of Staff continued:

-I will form a cape along this road, encircle, and attack from behind base 321! - This guy still loves the back-to-back fighting style.

Xuan Manh paced back and forth in the room, occasionally nodding his head as if he thought the Chief of Staff's opinion was in line with his own...

-One more detail! - The scout leader provides more. According to the report of two scout soldiers, the enemy force at base 321 belongs to the 415th division!

-This is so obvious! Ta Mok sent the 415th division up here on purpose. The 321 ridge had now become a key position in the region. From here they could expand their operations inland, around Bat Tam Bang town, reaching out to Bien Ho, directly threatening the government agency of Pailin district. At the same time, when the opportunity arose, he would jump into town!...The regiment commander put his hand under his chin, the beard of an ant that hadn't been shaved for two days had grown up. He glanced at the chief of staff.

- Who is the guy on road 10 in the South? The other day, the 2nd battalion reported that there were signs indicating that there could be an enemy base on the headwaters of the Sangke River, north of Samlot. Could that be the headquarters of Ta Mok? It's possible!

-Yes. We think so too! - The scout leader has zoned this area on the map for field inspection, so he hadn't reported it to the regiment commander.

Xuan Manh looked up and stared into the eyes of the chief of staff:

-Must find Ta Mok!...- That's an order.

Chapter 12

After three days, Tran Duy Chien returned from attending the "Celebration Congress," which was also the time his squad stationed at the 505 peak was replaced. Meeting his squad leader again in a neat and tidy uniform, with short hair and a handsome appearance, the soldiers surrounded him, asking all sorts of questions, to which Chien couldn't respond in time. First and foremost, everyone was concerned about their daily needs on the frontline:

-Where are my medicines?

-Where is my notebook?

-Did you remember to buy a razor?

And there was even the matter of "Have you visited the cemetery to pay respect to anyone?"...

Then, there were all sorts of discussions about things happening in heaven and on earth, and in the world and in the country. There was even talk about Thinh "wrinkle" at the Military Academy, and for over a year, many soldiers hadn't seen their "teacher." Chien returned to his unit, and everyone was happy because everyone had gained something from his trip. Chien returned just in time, and all year long, everyone was looking forward to this day: one person found a quiet place to smoke a filtered cigarette, inhaling deeply, swallowing the smoke into his chest, and exhaling slowly through his nostrils, feeling satisfied; another person shaved his chin, listening to the sound of the razor scraping against his skin, while others received books and stacks of paper, putting them in their backpacks to write letters to their friends and relatives at night...

For Chien, besides what he gained at the congress, he felt elated because he was able to help everyone with small tasks. Everyone was grateful that their squad leader had fully met their demands. Besides this shared joy, Chien had a great stroke of luck that his soldiers may not have known: he was still alive and unharmed after the vehicle he was in overturned on Route 10 this morning, narrowly escaping death, it seemed like he wouldn't have the chance to meet his comrades here again...

-Route 10 remains a constant danger, bringing disasters to Pailin. Many transport and armored vehicles passed by safely, but our vehicle hit a landmine right before the bridge in the Pang Ro Lin area. Fortunately, the GMC was only punctured and overturned on the roadside. We were thrown into the air like balls, and some of us fell to the ground. The driver suffered minor injuries and managed to crawl out. If it had hit two landmines like the last time, we would have all been done for. It's frightening to think of the roads here!...

The 3rd Battalion had been supplemented with a new group of soldiers. Ever since they set foot on the western front, this was the first group of rookies to be sent to Pailin. The convoy of vehicles transported the new soldiers and evacuated the wounded and dead to the rear, so ensuring safety along the way was of particular concern. There were dense patrols, checkpoints, and thorough reconnaissance of every inch of land, yet a mistake was made near a bend near the bridge, where no one expected. For Chiến, this trip was filled with a lot of luck and unforgettable memories. If it weren't for the sadness upon returning, he would probably be the luckiest and happiest person, not only in the 5th platoon but also in this 2nd company - a sadness that emanated from deep within when he just set foot back "home" and heard Chinh reporting the news, "Your Hill Myna is dead" ...

"Oh! Why did you leave me? Why didn't you wait for me to come back?" Chiến sat there listening to everyone telling the story of the hungry mice: "That night, it rained heavily, and the sudden cold air rushed into the checkpoint. The longer it rained, the heavier it got, the sky was dark, lightning flashed intermittently, and the wind grew stronger, causing the trees to sway and the ground to tremble, the water was pounding and stinging. Chinh stood under a tree, where Ngoc often sat on guard duty, covering himself with a raincoat. A lightning bolt struck the hilltop with a terrifying thunder. His Hill Myna in the cage shouted several times. Chinh thought the bird was worried about him, why he didn't come inside to get warm and avoid the cold? It reminded him twice like that. The rain just stopped, Chinh went into the bunker to put away his raincoat, looked over at the bird, and it was no longer in that cage. The cage hanging on the wall of the bunker was broken, missing several sticks, leaving a gap big enough for a hand to reach in. A few crickets that were saved for it were lying in an intact glass jar. Feeling that something was wrong with Hill Myna, Chinh searched the corners, fumbling and whistling, calling its name. Suddenly, Chinh collapsed when he saw his bird curled up in the corner of the bunker. Thinking that it was cold from the rain and wind, Chinh reached out to lift her up to his chest to warm it. Chinh jerked back, withdrawing his hand when he saw the bird's body covered in blood, its head separated from its neck. Chinh was stunned, screaming:

- Oh Ngoc! Dai! Come here quickly!...

Ngoc and Dai rubbed their eyes and ran over, witnessing the heartbreaking scene that had just happened to the Hill Myna on the peg. He urged Ngoc and Dai:

-Find the head of the bird right away, bring it back and bury it. The rats must have hidden its head somewhere!

Chính grieved:

- The hungry mice are the culprits. So much rice they had stolen from us at this checkpoint, and now they ruthlessly devour Hill Myna! What has the bird done wrong? Anh Chien, please forgive us. This is an unexpected situation, we never thought we would encounter a cunning and vicious mouse gang instead of the savage foxes we were prepared for. This mouse must have been huge to be able to bite off the bird's head and carry it away to hide!

At this moment, the atmosphere in the platoon sank as everyone recorded in their memory the death of Hill Myna on this treacherous land. Nhong had been with the volunteer soldiers for almost half a year and died because of the hungry mice...

Outside, the sun gradually dimmed as dark clouds covered half of it. It was time for Chien's platoon to put Hill Myna's matter aside and focus on their important tasks: the people who came to receive medicine, those who received papers and pens, and the things they were entrusted to buy. The matter of Hill Myna gradually faded away in the joy of those who were pleased after the platoon leader's trip. In the future, as time goes by and the fierce battle on this land continues, Hill Myna may never be mentioned again if it weren't for being recorded in the journal that Platoon Leader Tran Duy Chien wrote about his sorrow for Hill Myna's tragic death....

...Day... month... Year...

That's it! I'm so angry, angry at myself, angry at life, and furious with those stinky rats. I'm angry at myself for being too careless and irresponsible with my little beautiful Hill Myna friend, causing it to die. I'm angry at life for creating so many twists and turns that I had to be separated from my sparrow. I'm angry at those rats for eating my little bird and making me miss and mourn.

But who wouldn't miss and remember it? My beautiful sparrow was my friend, my source of great joy. Now it suddenly disappeared from my reach, and I couldn't help but feel nostalgic. What should I do? I blew my whistle with a nonchalant face, but now there's no sparrow flying to land on my shoulder anymore. My sparrow has died, and that's it! My nurturing and aspirations for my sparrow have now vanished. In the mornings, afternoons, and noon, I no longer catch insects for it to eat. That's it, my little sparrow has died. I miss and remember it so much!

However, every joy had its end, and every pain faded away with time. After a few days of rest, Chien returned with his team to work again. It had been a year since he stepped into military life, the young man from Quang wrote in his diary, *"I have become familiar with the hills and mountains/ Familiar with marching under heavy rain/ Familiar with the rhythmic steps of my small feet/ And have become accustomed to guns and bullets.*

On those journeys, Chien's small unit had four people gone, and four others came in to fill those "empty spaces." Those who fell were all close friends. Why do those who are deemed brave, compassionate, and hardworking have to go so soon? It's often the case, but sometimes it's not. The places Chien had witnessed death coming to anyone, at any time, for any reason: drowning in the rainy season, thirst in the dry season, fatal malaria, snake bites, eating poisonous mushrooms. But more than anything, it was death from mines and the traps of the enemy. The ones who had to die were anyone: the elderly, those who had never tasted the touch of a woman, those who had no one to carry on their legacy... Death was lurking everywhere, all the time on this hateful battlefield. Not only did the soldiers, the "good blacks, good reds" standing at the forefront of the waves and the wind, die haphazardly, die without being able to avoid it, but it happened every day, every month. In the back, where it was supposed to be safe, not only did the "privates" die but also the "generals" had people lying down, exhaling their last breath on this distant land. It's incomprehensible. It's incomprehensible, and there's no explanation, so people blame it on fate. When going on enemy searches, as soon as they stepped out of the house and saw the Turtle, some thought it was bad luck and wanted to turn back, but in the end, nothing happened. Another day, without encountering anything, Lam "deaf" died. The life of a soldier cannot rely on vague reasons to advance or retreat. According to Chien, as long as one is alive, one must fight, and when one dies, one returns to the earth, as no one can escape death. Suddenly, why was Chien so strong today, so dismissive of death? He opened his backpack and took out his diary to record this source of inspiration: "*Life only dies once, oh/ Die to be worthy of life/ I must stand tall, even if I have to die/ So that people will always remember, history will record my name.*"

Chapter 13

The recent convoy carrying new recruits up here was a victory. Unit 5 had been supplemented with nearly ten new soldiers. Each of them looked very young, with round and young faces, fluffy mouth.

- Soldiers like this, how can they fight?

When the two recruits arrived with their backpacks, the veterans immediately smiled. They spoke as if to encourage and comfort the two young soldiers:

"Weaker is better than lacking! We were just like you guys when we first arrived here. It took us five years to get used to it. Where are you guys from?"

"We're all from Quang Nam. An is from Que Son district, and my name is Tuan from Thang Binh!"

"We're all city people." Chiến pointed to Chinh and Ngoc standing next to him, and then assigned the team: "Chinh's team, together with An and Tuan, will assist Ngoc's team. My platoon will be divided into two teams, equipped with two B40s, one M60, and the rest AKs. Tomorrow, we will go on a search and destroy mission."

"What is a search and destroy mission, Chien?" A new soldier asked when he heard the platoon leader say that. He did not understand it. Previously, in books and on TV, they only talked about "the enemy sweeping", and had never heard of "search and destroy", or maybe "search and destroy" is also "sweeping". A veteran standing next to the platoon leader awkwardly replied,

- Search and destroy is... is... scouring the forest, and shooting when you encounter the enemy. Do you guys know how to shoot a gun?"

- We've learned up to the 'shooting from far and near' lesson!

- What about tactics? - Chien continued to ask.

"We've learned about 'individual and team combat maneuvers'!"

"Then that's good! You're better than us when we first arrived. During the Northeast Front, when the war broke out, we didn't finish the new soldier training program yet. The truck arrived at the barracks, and everyone jumped on, it was 'running and lining up', and we went to fight immediately. But you guys, even though you've learned the basic moves, it's still not enough in practice. Here, everyone has to be proficient in detecting and clearing mines!" Nguyen Van Chinh interrupted.

"We've also learned a little about mines, and grenades too!"

"Here, the enemy is dressed in black, sometimes visible and sometimes not, like 'wisps'. As for mines, there are too many to count, and we don't know where they get them to scatter in the forest! Remember, how the person in front walks, you must walk that way too, if you step on a mine carelessly, the least that can happen is losing one leg, if you encounter a mine, sometimes many people will be shot down!

Yesterday, while marching through the town, An looked through a hole in the canvas covering the front of the truck and saw that everyone here was wearing black clothes and scarves around their necks. Groups of people were shuffling along the road, walking under the blazing sun. There wasn't a single motorbike or car on the road, only military vehicles driving aimlessly. People said that under the rule of Pol Pot, cars, machinery, gold, silver, diamonds, and gems,... had been abandoned for several years. Cars, Honda motorcycles, and machinery were piled up in deserted villages, rusting and overgrown with weeds. After being liberated from the Khmer Rouge regime, people collected scrap, assembled and repaired a few bicycles. They only had the frame and wheels without tires, and they had to bend their backs and bounce over potholes and rocks, looking miserable. When An heard some old soldiers say that the enemy wore black clothes, An was a little skeptical:

-I see people wearing black clothes along the road! How can we know who the enemy is and who the innocent people are?!...

This question is really hard to answer. Mr Chinh stammered again:

-Uh... uh... yeah! This is difficult to distinguish. The day at Muong R'tay, when I was searching in a forest, I saw them rushing like a flock of ducks, men and women, all dressed in black. That day our regiment surrounded a forest, not a single escaped. It is true that among the hundreds of people that were destroyed, it is possible that some civilians, or soldiers' family members, ran after them. Because I heard that we killed over a hundred enemies but only got 80 guns!...

Outside, a young soldier who was cleaning a gun stopped to join the conversation:

-In order not to shoot at the wrong people, if someone shoots me, I shoot back. Whoever carries a gun is a Pot soldier!

-No! If so, then we will be passive. Those who do not carry guns can be members of the service such as carrying spears, loading bullets, auxiliary gunners of various types of firepower, or they shoot all bullets and then throw away their guns to run away?... These individuals are equally dangerous! There were a few foster brothers in the battalion who also picked up guns, even an 82mm mortar but didn't see a dead body next to them... In my opinion, just kill them all, except in the case of those who raise their hands to surrender. Of course, between the two bullets, someone can be wronged.!...

Heard that he was "unjustly wronged", a soldier from the Fourth area, a well-fed, well-dressed citizen said a sentence that he heard at home:

-Bulls and cows are sure, if they die unjustly, they will!
- (buffalos butts each other, flies and mosquitoes die unjustly – TG).

Right at the moment when the unit leader Tran Duy Chien came in from outside, he said as if to end the topic everyone was debating:

-There is no such thing in this area, only us and the enemy. The people here have all run to the town already!

Upon meeting for the first time, the conversation between the new soldiers and the veterans quickly turned into an exchange of experiences on the battlefield, as "learning from the master is not as good as learning from a friend". Despite appearing naive, the two new soldiers showed no signs of fear, which pleased Chiến, who nodded his head in satisfaction. He whispered to Chính and Ngọc, "This batch of recruits seems promising. Let's guide and teach them, who knows, they could become heroes someday!"

As the weather gradually transitioned into the rainy season, Cambodia was celebrating its traditional Chon Ch'nam Tho festival, which takes place between two seasons. The festival was a time of yearning for the heavens to grant rain to nourish all living beings, to bring back greenery to the land, and to allow fields to be cultivated and crops to be sown. It was a time for the fishes in Bien Ho (Tonle Sap) to thrive, and for the soldiers on the front lines to no longer have to worry about carrying bamboo tubes on their backs like they did during the dry season. Moreover, with the arrival of the rainy season, the enemy also took advantage of the weather to prolong their agony on this borderland.

Looking towards the mountain range to the west, which surrounded two-thirds of the valley, was similar to a mother embracing her injured child Pailin. In the south lies the peak of the mountain, where a diamond mine is located, resembling a mother's head with bright eyes illuminating the enemy's intentions. The imposing 505 ridge stood like a shoulder connecting two sturdy arms, supporting the powerful artillery ready to fire, like a fortress erected to welcome the sun and wind from the east, shielding the toxic winds from the west. The streams that flow down the mountain look as pure as a mother's milk nurturing the orphaned children of the Buddha's house, guarding the border of a distant land in the country of pagodas day and night...

Chapter 14

Regarding Battalion Commander Ngo Xuan Manh, whenever he receives letters from family, friends or official documents sent down, he always carefully uses a pair of scissors to cut a line close to the edge of the envelope, then uses two fingers to grip the paper and pull it out. This gesture shows that he is a careful person. Today, perhaps due to impatience, Xuan Manh did not do so. He tilted the envelope, tapped it a few times on the table to make the paper inside gather to one side, and tore it along the edge of the envelope to retrieve the letter. A piece of graph paper with his wife's handwriting was torn from his son's first-grade notebook. She wrote:

My beloved husband,

It's been a long time since we heard from you, and we miss you very much. When I heard Tuat talk about the situation over there, I became very worried. I know you're going through hardships, struggling and lacking, and there's nothing I can do to help you.

Our child is still healthy and attending school regularly. Last month, he ranked third, one rank lower than before. Maybe because of the changing weather, he had a cold for a few days. Now he's better, so don't worry!

The other day, some colleagues over there came over to visit my mother and our child, and then went to the Youth Union's office to do something before registering for the flight back to the unit next week...Today, when you receive this letter from me, maybe they have already gone over there...

Putting his wife's letter on the table, Xuan Manh paused for a moment, his eyes looking towards an undefined distant place. The Battalion Commander asked his subordinate:

-Do you know who came to our house just now?!

Tuat recalled and replied:

-Looks like the guys in the political department! That day, I had just arrived when the uncles came out from the house. They went a few days ahead of me, your wife didn't have time to write a letter, so she sent it to me today to bring it to you!

-I see!... Xuan Manh blurted out. Tuat was bewildered, not understanding what his boss said:

-Is something wrong, uncle?!

- Oh, it's nothing!

The commander continued reading his wife's letter:

... "I still haven't been able to get a job, dear! To become a teacher here, I need to have city residency, a recommendation letter from a school outside of the North, I have to bring those papers from our hometown, and go through many other procedures. It's also very expensive to even just get your foot in the door here. Maybe I have to give up on this profession! For now, I'll collect recyclables and spend time taking care of our child...

The winds from the plain blow up, carrying the warmth of the dry season, dispersing the vague clouds on the hillside as if regretting something that doesn't want to fly away, revealing the vast green forest of the Pailin mountain region. The sun rises high, the pale yellow morning light spreading evenly on the lawn in front of the yard, glittering droplets of dew that still linger from the night like strings of pearls. A faint sadness suddenly appears on the wrinkled, dark face of the battalion commander...

Xuan Manh knew that Party Committee Binh had sent someone to the rear to investigate the cause of a soldier's disappearance on the border last month. Binh believed that this was related to an illegal human trafficking organization in which his wife was a link. But he didn't care, "let them do it, the truth is what matters." Xuan Manh put on his glasses and read his wife's letter. The scribbled lines danced before his eyes:

... *"The other day there were some soldiers, I don't know from which unit, but they asked me for directions to the other side, I just told them to register for a flight. Then I didn't see them come back...".*

Xuan Manh's thoughts were in turmoil. Binh's scheme to undermine him by sending spies to investigate had left him wondering about the fate of the soldiers who had been sent. He couldn't help but wonder if the rumors were true, and if his wife had taken money and gold to help the soldiers cross the border illegally. He believed his wife wouldn't do so. But what if it was the truth? In times of desperation, anything could happen... Xuan Manh was famous for his calm and collected exterior, always keeping the internal relationships balanced, even when there was a critical and dangerous situation, people did not see any expression called confusion, fear or worry on the face of the Regiment Commander. However in this case, Xuan Manh was feeling anything but calm inside, causing him to be truly confused. He was worried about his family and felt helpless in his inability to do anything for them. His frustration and anger were building, but he didn't know who to direct it towards. All he wanted was to know the truth. Just then, his wife's letter arrived in time.

Amidst the stillness of the night, a sudden explosive loud noise jolted. Xuan Manh emerged from the door and scanned the neighboring house before grabbing his flashlight and heading towards the operations bunker where Thanh was still wide awake. Despite the late hour, Thanh remained engrossed in the map laid out across two-thirds of the makeshift table fashioned from ammo boxes, with a pot of "He Shou Wu" tea by his side. Back in the countryside, Thanh savored a cup of fragrant Thai Nguyen green tea paired with a few sweet potatoes in place of rice. However, since coming to the battlefield, without Thai Nguyen green tea, he had forgotten the taste of his favorite meal. Luckily, Thanh discovered an abundance of He Shou Wu trees in the red soil of Pailin and had someone uproot them to bring back. He dried and packed them into bags, replacing his beloved Thai Nguyen green tea with this new drink, he even sent some to the battalions to boil for the soldiers. Thanh's devotion to his daily He Shou Wu ritual earned him the nickname "Thanh He Shou Wu" amongst his comrades.

The chief strategist was perfecting the plan to launch an offensive against the enemy stronghold. The eyes of the strategist officer sank into the darkness, his hands tightly gripping the pens, causing their face to contort. Looking up at the enemy's tactical map - with our sharp arrowheads, viewers could sense the location of "Thanh He Shou Wu." It not only demonstrated the skill and professionalism of the offensive ideology but also affirmed the command's determination to attack the enemy. They said that the arrowhead on the map represents the commander's abilities, the fighting spirit, tactics, and battlefield experience. The commander's aptitude was contained within the arrows on the battlefield map, and by looking at them, one can predict the outcome of a campaign or a battle. Through checking the strategist officer's work, the talent of an individual can be found within the arrows and lines. The battalion commander was fond of the arrows of the chief strategist, Thanh. In the "Battle Plan," Xuan Manh would always find the small but powerful red arrows hidden among countless military symbols, which could change the situation from danger to opportunity and from difficulty to ease. These were the arrows that aimed at the enemy's weak spots or rear flank.

-I am still not confident about this!" The regiment commander pointed the antenna rod at the red arrow, while Thanh drew a line like a silk strip crossing the border with a sharp nose like a bird's beak. Two frontal rods, despite the complex obstacles that need to be overcome, are still more reassuring on "our land". If the attack is not finished, it can be left for the next day. As for this arrow (Xuan Manh pointed to the deep arrow), besides having to go through the minefield, it also has to penetrate deep into the other side, nearly a kilometer away. Will there be any problems? Until now, there has been no clear policy allowing crossing the border. I believe that if a report is submitted to request opinions, no one will agree. We need to take the initiative in this matter, and if we leave one or two platoons behind, it will be very troublesome! Of course, we are ready to take responsibility, but we must also consider the lives of our comrades and the impact on diplomatic work! ...

The chief advisor Thanh put down the colored pencil and looked up at the battalion commander:

- Oh my god! For the enemy, even if we don't capture prisoners of war, even if we don't collect the enemy's bodies, they will still find something to twist. They are accusing Vietnam of invading, is that true? I'm telling you, anyone who is afraid to cross that hostile border and fears the impact on diplomatic work should go home and be a househusband. Diplomacy is also a battlefield, and we have to fight fiercely. To win on the diplomatic front, we must win on the battlefield. In this battle, I suggest we move this arrow over here to create a surrounding position, cutting off from behind. But if we attack head-on, we might as well prepare for defeat. Do you see this arrow I drew with one of the other arrows? This is also implementing the Party Committee's resolution of *"Mastering the thought-offending, forming-encirclement-from-side-and-behind, hit-fast, hit-to-destroy, master-of-the-field, take prisoners, collect weapons, lower the casualty rate, handle well-policy-injury-injury-killers...".*

Thanh spoke with a clear voice, as if he were addressing the battalion commander directly, saying, "I'm telling you, I have evidence to back up what I'm saying!" Seeing the chief of staff so enthusiastic, Regiment Commander Xuan Manh felt as though they were sharing a common purpose. Though he didn't say it out loud, he believed that Thanh was referring to Binh... who had been staunchly opposed to sending troops across the border. Every night, Binh would tune in to the BBC to hear about the ongoing war in Cambodia. When he heard that a Vietnamese soldier had been captured by Thai border guards in the west of Pailin, it exacerbated the already existing tensions between him and the regiment commander, as well as some of the other officers in the unit. Binh felt marginalized and isolated while the role of the regiment commander was becoming more prominent like a flag in the storm. He then speculated that the incident was due to Xuan Manh's wife, who was based in the rear, establishing connections that enabled her husband to smuggle people across the border in exchange for money and gold. Binh had heard from an assistant, who had conducted an investigation upon returning to the rear, that "there were some soldiers, not from our battalion, who got permission to fly back to the front. They knew the battalion commander's wife had many connections, so they visited her and asked for her help in returning to the front by military aircraft!" The reason why this was such a big deal was that there was only one supply and wounded soldier transport flight per week. If soldiers could fly back to the front, it would be a blessing instead of having to travel thousands of miles by car, which was both exhausting and dangerous.

Secretary Binh was both regretful and remorseful. He regretted that his past actions, which lacked wisdom and tact, had exposed his true unscrupulous nature to some people, which was devaluing the reputation of others to elevate his own status. Perhaps he was able to climb the ranks to become the deputy political commissar of a battalion thanks to the disciplinary violations of his subordinates while he was a supervisory officer, and now he was hoping for the outcome of an investigation into an illegal border crossing incident to help him ascend to a higher position. Therefore, when he heard the inspector's report, Binh was disappointed. But he didn't stop there and turned his attention to pursuing another case. In front of the assistant, he said:

- I monitor the Western broadcasts, and there was another case of one of our soldiers crossing the border that happened last month. Check to see if there is anyone missing from the battalions?!

The assistant frowned, pondered for a moment, and remembered:

- Last month, there were two cases. One soldier from the 1st battalion crossed over to the enemy side, got lost for seven days, and reported back upon his return. He didn't eat or drink for seven days, was chased relentlessly, and came back on the eighth day, with torn clothes and full of injuries. That was really close! He deserves to be nominated as a hero by the state!

- What's his name? Why didn't I hear the report? - Binh cut off the political assistant.

- His name is Hung. We usually call him Hung "black"! The staff already reported it! The second case was Mai, the scout. He went to capture the enemy but was ambushed and killed in the Parrot's Beak area, and his body couldn't be retrieved!

Deputy Political Commissar Binh felt like he was unnecessary, with so many important incidents, yet no one reported them. The next day, he summoned the heads of departments and agencies to a meeting and scolded them severely, saying: "Do you think I'm just an average person?! How can I lead if this is the case? Are you still officials and party members?" Everyone was dumbfounded and suddenly summoned and reprimanded.

"Please inform us, sir, what has happened!"

"So many cases of injuries, casualties, disappearances, and disciplinary violations... Why didn't you report them to me?"

As his professional responsibility was questioned, the military assistant stood up and said:

-There is a daily summary and report during the briefing. Every day we have a summary report in the meeting. Each specific case we report according to the relevant industry!

Maybe Binh has already heard it, there's no meeting without the Party Secretary's presence, but maybe he forgot due to being too busy. He added one last sentence to end the meeting:

-Report everything to me, no matter what subjects. Got it?...

And today, amidst the last few days of the rainy season, the battalion is preparing for the dry season combat plan. At this time, political commissar Truong Thanh Binh was ordered back to the front office after a period of practical experience. Binh had been present at the Cambodian battlefield since the hot days of the southwestern border, mainly working at the front office. His time in the field as a party secretary at the battalion level had taught him valuable lessons. "*Indeed! Party work - Political work at the frontline office is very different from that in other units, between schools and battlefields, between theory and distant practice. Fulfilling the duties of an officer at the front office only takes a little sweat, time, and a bunch of knowledge acquired from school. A secretary, political commissar at a combat battalion must also be closely linked to the bones and blood of many soldiers' fates (!)."*

Truong Thanh Binh sat in a dim corner of the room, lost in thought for hours. The flickering oil lamp cast his distorted shadow on the swaying wall, as if he were deep in contemplation. Where was he, he wondered? Had his actions caused all the trouble since he arrived? Had he been too confident in himself and ignored the opinions of those around him? He had helped the battalion commander accomplish the mission in the past, but why did people seem to avoid him now? Why? Why? If someone had seen Binh's face at this moment, they would have noticed his remorse. But it was too late, far too late. Binh had wasted a rare opportunity to prove himself to everyone and his superiors. It wasn't until the last minute, as he prepared to leave the front and return to headquarters, that he realized everything. "I'll apologize to the regiment commander," he thought. To effect a change in himself, words were not enough. Binh had finally realized that his perspective, cognition, and actions had to undergo a "decoding" process based on the debates in the battalion. Then, why would a person with an ironclad perspective like Binh lower himself to the decision of "apologizing to the regiment commander and everyone" before putting on his backpack and returning to the paper battlefield, unless it was the blood and bones of a soldier...

As the night on the border grew later, it became quieter and colder. A bright star broke away from the sky, leaving a long trail in the universe before disappearing.

The wild rooster crowed. Another day began between two battlefronts.

Chapter 15

In order to protect the town of Pailin on this land of death, besides keeping the vital road from the town of Battambang to here always clear, it is necessary to first uproot the thorn "321". If this problem could not be solved, upcoming rainy season should be cautious. To the north of base 321 was Com Riem, an important connection in the system of border bases between Cambodia and Thailand, west of Battambang province. However, the base directly threatening Pailin was base 321. Com Rieng was also important, but it was a bit far from Pailin and separated by the Mong Con Bo Ray River, which was over two hundred meters wide. Therefore, regiment commander Xuan Manh and chief of staff Thanh urgently completed the plan to attack base 321. Around this high point and the entire border area stretching up to Com Riem for tens of kilometers, there were dense forests of wood and thick ken bamboo. Perhaps the history of this area had been disputed with neighboring countries in the past, so people planted thorny bamboo to prevent enemies. The strength of thorny bamboo was resilient and more durable than any other type of tree. When the bamboo was old, it sprouted new shoots, or when the bamboo tree was burned, the root shoots out many new bamboo shoots. The more it was cut down, the more sharp thorns it grew to resist the destroyer. People used this "self-defense" law to make natural barriers, like it protected itself. The ancients had a saying: "Cutting bamboo is hardest, second is flirting a girl"... These were not easy tasks. Nowadays, the matter of thorns is like "daily business", while thorny bamboo would always be thorny bamboo. Knowing the complex nature of the terrain in this area, especially the dangerous high point 321, "Thanh He Shou Wu" proposed to battalion commander Manh that besides the two main fronts from the east, when attacking 321, it was necessary to form a rear attack. However, the Party Committee Binh strongly opposed it. Thanh believed that Binh's disagreement was an obstacle from within. Binh explained: "

-With this combat object, annihilation is just an illusion! No matter how many marks and how many directions he circled, he couldn't encircle such a large base. Does their firepower from above allow you to attack so easily? There are also natural obstacles interspersed with mines like the armor that surrounds the base! Add to that the adverse weather, the rainy season is here! Three factors to win, two factors have been lost are: "favorable geographical and environmental conditions"!...

-"So what is your rationale?" - Someone asked the Secretary again.

Binh was momentarily confused because he had not prepared his viewpoint, but then he regained his composure and said:

"If we have multiple directions, our forces will be dispersed and hindered in overcoming obstacles. We should focus on one strong direction to break through, combining with high-density firepower to occupy the top of the hill. The enemy will not be able to withstand it and will have to surrender. Once we have secured the high ground, we will not only relieve the pressure of the enemy on the North Pailin direction, but also force their bases along the border to move out of our range of fire!..."

Binh's opinion had various aspects that made everyone here think. Thanh did not want the regiment commander to speak up because he had proposed a multi-directional attack plan that Binh had rejected, so the Chief of Staff asked:

"Is the Secretary being subjective? If we organize a breakthrough in one direction and it fails, what then? In warfare, as in other fields, there must be two plans, and the use of force must also have a reserve force, let alone a battle like this with so many disadvantages!"

"If this guy is married, he will likely have a mistress, a reserve wife!" - someone sitting in the back poked fun at "Thanh He Shou Wu", causing laughter in the meeting room. The Chief of Staff turned around and said seriously:

"I am serious. We have to prepare for all possible situations. If we have only one plan, we are not guaranteed to win!"

Binh was brave in his arguments:

- In battle, any situation can occur. But here, we need to assess the actual situation in this area and in this battle to bring out creativity in our tactics! The lessons learned from experience have been documented, we're not here to lecture, but we're also not here to experiment. We must see that this is for victory and for the bones and blood of our troops. On the other hand, the policy of the two states is to achieve military victory that meets political requirements! ... Binh still disagrees with the deployment of troops beyond the border.

After many hours, the discussion on the battle plan turned into a debate on academia and strategic principles. Of course, fighting the enemy is not a game. The soldiers needed to present all the basic principles and their application under specific conditions to choose the optimal plan. Optimal meant scientifically considering how to achieve victory while minimizing our losses. They did not consider the factor of chance. The meeting did not seem to reach a high level of agreement because there were opposing views even among the command and leadership of the battalion.

At the end of the meeting, Regiment Commander Xuan Manh did not take a vote, which is like an "art of leadership" in his behavior. In some ways, a vote is just a formality, and it could lean towards the plan proposed by the chief of staff, but it was not totally agreed upon and did not reflect the strong determination of a regiment party and would make it harder for Binh.

However, Xuan Manh still reported the plan to the commander, but also clearly stated differing opinions:

"Any disaster caused to Pailin from here, from this base!" - Xuan Manh pointed to point 321. The reconnaissance battalion crawled all the way there, with about a platoon, possibly the special forces of the 415th division, few but with an advantage. The entire division and warehouse system are scattered, stretching along the border line up to Com Reng. From this expenditure checkpoint, they can send troops across Route 58 into the interior, destroying the economic and political bases of the revolutionary government in Bat Tam Bang province. Some of our units were recently attacked by them, and they may be the culprits! ...

At the forward command post, the division commander came in and out, his hair turning silver, his eyes scanning the battle plan map. He had been thinking for a long time:

- Beware of their schemes. We have shed so much blood and bones around this valley already. Are they really eager to regain Pailin as we predicted, or do they have some other sinister motive? ... We must not lose Pailin while we are here. But we cannot let the blood flow any more! We need to reconsider what Tà Mok wants.

The political commissar agreed:

- Losing Pailin is impossible, but will the blood stop flowing when the enemy still exists daily, hourly, with bases still clinging around while our operations are not enough to eliminate them?

After the political commissar finished speaking, Xuan Manh continued his report:

- We have prepared a plan to attack base 321. If we achieve this goal, not only will we eliminate the danger threatening Pailin, but we will also prevent their infiltration into the interior!

- No 'if' whatsoever. We must solve it immediately! - The division commander interrupted the battalion commander. He was the strictest commander on this northwest front. His temperament was purely from Quang Tri, and when he was hot, even iron and steel would melt, and when he was cold, water would freeze into ice. His revolutionary spirit of attack was unquestionable, but he "remembers for a long time, remembers every detail" of those who often disobey orders. Then he made the decision: "You must find Tà Mok's whereabouts. If he is still here, this area will remain unsafe!

The captain looked straight into Xuan Manh's eyes:

- The fact that we have to establish this base is a result of not deploying our forces to control the area in the past. This is your responsibility!

Xuan Manh understood this, but not everything that is understood can be done. There is a gap between thinking and acting, if not to say that a revolution in military thinking is needed here. The debates in the conferences, the blood and sweat of the soldiers, have completely overturned the conservative mindset in Truong Thanh Binh...

Chapter 16

The Division Command summoned the commanders of all the forces on the Western front to the headquarters. Upon receiving the message, Xuan Manh was unsure of what to expect. It was rare for the Division to hold meetings at times like this. It was the peak season and the Division's operational range was extensive, covering the entire Bat Tam Bang province, as well as the Batia Meanchey province to the north and the Pua Sat province to the south. "There must be something important going on," Xuan Manh thought to himself as he grabbed his bag and set out. It took a whole company of soldiers to escort someone to a Division meeting - they needed to mobilize an infantry battalion, armored vehicles, engineering units, and guards. It was like a military campaign. The situation was urgent. As soon as Xuan Manh stepped into the headquarters, the battalion commander met him and led him to the conference room.

- Don't underestimate Ta Mok. He is a daring commander who often surprises his opponents with things that are not in the textbooks. The worst are the fools, who tend to be crazy when they're stupid!" warned Colonel Le Tu. Since we left the Northeast front and came here, the enemy has changed their strategy from retreating to stopping to defend. This will be a prolonged fight, and we might have to pay a heavy price!" Le Tu traced a curved line along the border. The enemy had established military bases disguised as refugee camps: Cao Me Lai - O Da, Com Rieng - 321 - Ta Sanh... he pointed at each target. They fought us using guerrilla tactics, but these bases were not guerrilla bases - they were a basic defense system for the defeated army to survive. Pailin is now a target on the Western front that they are aiming for. One of the three targets will be the focus of intense fighting across the entire Northwest front: Pailin, Ampin, and Ang Long Veng!...

Until now, Xuan Manh had always thought that his battalion was an independent unit on one side of the front. And indeed, at the beginning of 1979, he brought his battalion up here to take over Pailin from a border unit, and stayed there "without a specific deadline." Many soldiers from the rear had stepped on the trucks, covered in tarpaulins, and after a few days of driving, they arrived here, making friends with the jungle and the grass. After two or three years, they would ride the trucks back to the rear, with all kinds of illnesses and injuries. They only heard of Cambodian women wearing sarongs, having wide hips and wearing headscarves, but they didn't know how they looked. Now Pailin was one of the key targets on the northwest front.

Since the day when unit 1 was deployed to build a stronghold in the direction of the northern town, the situation has not improved much, and now a new artillery base has appeared on high ground 321. Today, when Regiment Commander Xuan Manh looked at the map at the division headquarters, he was startled to see two more bases near Pailin in the north: Salak'rao and Com Rieng. Division Commander Le Tu said:

- Ta Mok has also considered the possibility that we may attack base 321, so he has set up these two bases to form a stronghold: 321 - Com Rieng - Salak'rao, to both support base 321 and narrow the encirclement around Pailin. He is indeed an old fox! Before the rainy season comes, we must solve this target! - Le Tu pointed to high ground 321 and looked up at Xuan Manh. But attacking now is impossible because Com Rieng and Salak'rao are still there. If we attack all three targets at the same time, we will be fools. The book has taught us that when many enemies appear at the same time, we must concentrate our strength to overwhelm and "defeat one enemy" so that the other "two enemies" will fall without fighting. Com Rieng may be the first target!...

Xuan Manh looked at Le Tu's mouth talking, but at this moment, he was thinking about another issue. Since the division commander mentioned the name Ta Mok, he considered it his responsibility to find his whereabouts. After the meeting, Xuan Manh went to the provincial military expert team. The team leader, Nam Hung, was a tall, almost oversized man in a summer military uniform. He had an open mind and spoke kindly. Among the people over 60 years old on the front lines at that time, Nam Hung looked the sharpest. He and the provincial chairman, Bat Tam Bang Key Kim Giang, were inseperable, intimate like father and son. For Xuan Manh, Nam Hung was a close and friendly person due to the years he had spent together on the international battlefield in Bat Tam Bang province. Seeing Xuan Manh from outside, holding a stick, walking in, Nam Hung stepped out and said jokingly:

-Where did you get lost? I'm also waiting to meet you!

-Can you tell me the reason why you want to meet me first to see if it matches the purpose of my coming here?

- Then tell me your purpose first. Now I'm the host, you are the guest. "Guest is King"!

-But we still maintain the "host first, guest second" mechanism in our country, don't we?

-Really? Have a tea - The head of the expert group poured two glass cups and invited the "guest" to drink tea with for a few Cambodian phrases that he usually communicated with the local people. Nam Hung lowered his voice enough for the two of them to hear: "During the Chon Ch'nam Tho Lunar New Year, did a delegation from the province visit and give gifts to the children?"

-That day, the provincial delegation, consisting of nearly ten people, including a woman as the head of the delegation, collaborated with Pailin district. After the delegation returned, we breathed a sigh of relief.

We were afraid of the dangers along the way and didn't know how to deal with any issues that might arise.

-Is it Nari, by any chance?

-She's a female official in the commune! - Xuan Manh hesitated, looking at Nam Hung and answering.

-You know her? The province is going to transfer her to the Commission's office. She's almost thirty and looks charming and intelligent! When did you meet her? - Nam Hung smirked, hiding a subtle smile, but Xuan Manh also recognized that smile, so he only told part of the truth:

-I only met her recently. During the advance to Pailin, I met her in a Phum. In the early days, people here appreciated the soldiers a lot. They called the Vietnamese voluntary troops "the army of the Buddha." After a while, I unexpectedly met her again during the recent Lunar New Year! ...- In fact, Mạnh had visited Nari many times.

-Have you done anything with her yet? - Nam Hung asked a question that only those involved would understand.

Xuan Manh knew that Nam Hung was teasing him, but it coincided with a memory when he first came to this area and could hardly forget the moment between him and Nari. When they met, before saying goodbye, Manh forgot the Cambodian custom of clasping hands together in front of his chest, so he held Nari's warm and soft hand, keeping it in his hand for a long time.

Nari felt awkward and didn't want to pull her hand away from his, so she had to use words:

-When you return to the town, please come to my house to visit! ...- While speaking, Nari gently withdrew her hand from Xuan Manh's.

-Yes, thank you, Nari, I will come!

-I'll be waiting for you. Don't disappoint me! ...

From there, Nari's figure appeared and disappeared, constantly lingering in the mind of Regiment Commander Ngo Xuan Manh. This morning, he visited Nari. Nari's house is near the main road, next to the village council. Her family was also a victim of the genocide regime. Her father and older brother fled to become soldiers and were killed. She was teaching in the city when a political incident occurred and she was pushed to the Pailin mountainous region with her mother, who worked on the Battambang field. Fortunately for her and the people here, the volunteer army units arrived in time to help the people in this border area. That day, the enemy invaded the village, taking all the men, women, and children to the border. The group was wading through the Sang Ke river to cross to the other side when the enemy's remnants were intercepted by the 3rd Battalion's pursuit force, blocking them in the middle of the flowing water. The terrified Khmer Rouge soldiers ran away. Xuan Manh ordered a company, including a medic, to carry the old people and carry the children across the river, bringing them all back to the village, treating the sick, and providing food and rice to those who were hungry and exhausted, some of whom had fainted from hunger. In the following days, Manh mobilized his forces to help the people rebuild houses, schools, and provide medical care and medicine for the people. He told his troops:

- We will stay here for a long time, there is no certain place to rely on to complete our mission outside of the people here. Protecting and helping them is one of our main purposes!

Since then, Xuan Manh hadd often come here, both to inspect and to build relationships with the revolutionary government, including coordinating with local guerrillas to fight together. Whatever comes, will come. In their working relationships, Xuan Manh had sensed something from the woman named Nari, who was often awkward, shy, and blushing every time she met him. And then, in the face of Nari's sincerity and modest gestures, there were moments that made the regiment commander of the Vietnamese voluntary army's heart flutter... Romantic relationships between two people of different genders often had their own signals, expressed through eye contact, smiles, the first handshake, and even in vague words, exchanging and then all creating the lightning that breaks down all barriers between two extremes...

Seeing Xuan Manh coming, Nari hurried out to greet him. She didn't know what to do at this moment.

- Does your mother have a house, Nari? – Xuan Manh took the initiative to ask to relieve her awkward gesture.

- Yes. My mom is pruning corn outside. Let me call her in. She keeps asking about you. She will be very happy to meet you!"

Nari went inside to call her mother from the back door. Xuan Manh followed behind and suddenly called out, "Nari!"

Nari turned around and it was when Manh came close to her and hugged her. It seemed like Nari wasn't prepared, she felt surprised. Nestled in the arms of the volunteer army officer, she felt excited, her chest pounding. Nari stood still, her body soft and weak, her feet seemed to want to bend down, she had to lean on Xuan Manh to avoid falling. Her breasts were pressed firmly against his chest. Her full and beautiful face looked up, her eyes half-closed waiting for him...

"Oh! You!"

"Nari, my dear!..."

"Yes! Oh my god, I'm dying!... Oh... oh..."

Xuan Manh kissed her lips, her cheeks, her neck, reached into Nari's pants and shirt, and then bit the round bosom with two pink nipples, each piece of flesh on his body curled up and stiffened... Nari endured it all, the world spinning like a merry-go-round, her limbs no longer moving, letting go. The two of them rolled onto the bed beside them...

Outside, the wind was blowing and slamming against the door. The dark clouds had appeared out of nowhere, covering the sun and turning the space dark, soothing the scorching heat of the harsh dry season that was raging here... Back in the house, the corrugated iron sheets banging against each other woke the two up from their stupor...

"I have important news for you!" the team leader of the experts continued. The sudden fleeting memories of Xuan Manh about the girl were immediately interrupted by the loud voice of Nam Hung.

"I'm listening!"

"Among the delegates who came to celebrate Tet that day, the base reported that there was a 'two-faced' enemy infiltrator!"

"Did they reveal the name and unit?"

"The name doesn't matter to them. In this newly reborn country, no agency has been able to identify the identity of each citizen like ours. In my opinion, the main thing is to know which unit it belongs to, where it operates, and who commands him?"

"Those are the things we urgently need to know. Can you give me more specific information? That's the purpose of my visit this time!"

"You need to contact the military intelligence agency for specific information. I'm only telling you that this person can know a lot about the area around Pailin... If you go there, we'll have a meeting with the provincial team this afternoon!"

Xuan Manh didn't want to face him directly. He thought that he was a target that Tà Mok was looking for, so it would be better to get information through the military intelligence agency. But then he decided to exploit him directly. He went straight to the intelligence department:

"I want to question this person with you!"

"Ta Mok assigned him to investigate your command headquarters! You shouldn't face him!"

"I've met him before. He knows me!"

The military intelligence officer widened his eyes.

"How?"

"During Tet, he came with the provincial delegation to visit us in Pailin!"

"And after returning, the provincial police arrested him!" The head of military intelligence revealed.

"It's excellent of you guys to know him!"

"We have confidential sources. Alright, let's go meet him!"

Chapter 17

Division commander Le Tu decided to attack the enemy base at the 321 ridge, but he did not assign it to the 3rd Regiment, he assigned it to another force that came to carry out. The battle was unsuccessful, it was rather a defeat, because not only did they not control the target, but also left dozens of lives there... Ta Mok, the notoriously evil, devious and crafty commander jumped up, ran across the border like a madman. He summoned his subordinates to a meeting to celebrate the victory.

- I knew it, the "Duon" would surely attack 321. Our firepower from here was firing down on them all day and night, like a thorn in the eye, they must pull it off!- He was proving why the enemy has to "hang the shirt" around this dangerous ridge, maybe they had fallen for his plan - I have planted mines around the hillside, and there are very few people on it. I have prepared to sacrifice a few "pawns", mainly as bait for them. At the same time, a small force of us managed the secret path from the top, anyone who ran away without permission could be shot. Our battlefields and mortars lied still, taking the exact element. At eight o'clock, "the Duon" fired a few shells and then jumped up and took over it easily. Oh ho! They fell for my plan… While they were in the mood, you know what, a rain of our mortars covered the top of the hill. There were no fortifications on it. Before that, I did not allow people to build fortifications or trenches at all. Now you know… Oh my god, the dead, the injured, screaming, the view when standing on the observatory looks spectacular!… 321 did the right job as a "meat mill". In the future it may be lost like Com Rieng, but we have achieved the main goal of destroying the enemy's forces!…

They all sat and listened, eyes wide in admiration of Ta Mok's tactical talent. He was excited, passionately continued: "They frantically drifted down the hillside to avoid mortar fire, wherever they went, the mines exploded there. We didn't need to attack, nearly a company had already perished around the hillside. So I ordered the mortars, just shoot on it, don't need much, don't stand in one place, this position they shoot a few shells, move to another battlefield to shoot a few, their 105 cannons are not like a rifle, cannot calculate the element in time. I made my people shoot like that, until the darkness covered their eyes, blocking all of their actions. So they had to leave everything around that mountain: the dead, the wounded and even the guns…Who dares to go in there and bring it out, will be bait for wild boars, iguanas and wolves!.. .".

The dry season was over. When the gunfire stopped, the rain poured down. 321 Ridge remained as it was. But so many souls of soldiers were wandering, writhing in pain during the rainy season…

For more than a week now, Tran Duy Chien had been tormented by malaria, he had a fever once every one day. When he was at home, his mother said it was a "once-every-one-day fever". Every time he had a fever, his mother cooked a pot of scallion porridge. After he finished the bowl of porridge, his mother put him on the bed and covered him with a tight blanket from head to toe. Sweat drenched his clothes and soaked into the blanket. When he couldn't stand it anymore, Chien threw the blanket away, and his mother wiped his body with a towel, then squeezed out a cup of water. Doing so twice would completely cure him, then he went out into the yard to see why he was so light that day. Another time, when the weather changed due to seasonal change, he had a fever, his mother changed his treatment "regimen" by giving him onion porridge and making him take a steambath at the same time. She picked all kinds of leaves: eucalyptus, bamboo leaves, lemongrass leaves, lemon leaves, wormwood... and put them in a pot, covered the lid, boiled it till it bubbled, then made Chien sit with his back hunched over the pot, his mother brought a blanket to cover his whole body and the pot of steamed leaves. Before pressing Chien's head down so that his face was close to the mouth of the pot, his mother opened the lid and put a lump of balm in it. Oh my god, at the bottom, the hot steam from the pot rose to the face, above, his mother's hands pressed the head down. Chien could not raise his head, he had to open the blanket close to the floor to let the wind in. After a while, his mother poked her chopsticks into the pot to stir the steam, and continued to press down her son's head. So he was cured. At this age, Chien had never stepped foot in the hospital, nor had he ever been injected with quinine. Today, if he had been at home, Chien would also have been enjoying a bowl of onion porridge and being cared for by his mother's hand. After a week of lying on the bamboo stall, Chien sat up and took a few steps, but he had a splitting headache, he was dizzy and was about to fall when sitting down and standing up. I must have been severely anemic, he thought. However, when he recovered from the fever, he wanted to eat a lot. Malaria consumed energy very quickly. The time after the fever was over, the body needed to replenish the lost energy because it had to fight the malaria parasite, otherwise it would continue to overpower him. Everyone knew that, but there was nothing here to foster. In the company, there were a few cases that turned into malignancy, hematuria that could not be cured in time. Huddled himself up in a hammock, Chien crossed his arms over his forehead, an endless sadness invaded his soul, he was sad for the soldier's miserable fate. Right now, if he was at home, there would be a mother's warm hand on his forehead, and then that same hand scooped spoons of onion porridge into her son's mouth like a little bird lying in a nest opening its mouth to be fed by its mother. Oh, thinking about that, tears welled up in his eyes, rolling down his cheeks. When people were sick, lying alone, they often thought about the past, when they lived in full materiality they often had unrealistic dreams. If people were currently sick and needy, people often felt sorry for themselves, complained about their fate, why they were so unlucky...

Someone's voice was heard from afar along with the wind blowing in, Chien stood up when Chinh was returning from a meeting in the company, stopping by to report to the squad leader:

- Tomorrow, our squad will sweep the North of the coffee plantation. You just woke up with a fever, stay home for a few days to get well, let me take charge of the squad instead!

- Thanks Chinh! Perhaps you are the one who understands me better than anyone. However, I can't stay at home while you guys are pouring blood, sweat and tears. I will go with you guys!

- No! You can't go yet, you just woke up from a fever, you will have a fever when you go out!

- I still know that, but if I don't go, people will misunderstand that I am hiding at home, it's very embarrassing!

- That's my advice, go or not, it's up to you. Sick, old, no one judges a person who has just woken up!

Among the common diseases, malaria caused people to lose strength the fastest. Chien was as green as a leaf, but he still refused to stay at home. This time, Chien's squad was sent to the North of the coffee plantation to work to prevent the enemy from breaking into Pailin town after our army's 321 Ridge attack failed. Preparing to depart, Chien asked his brothers:

- Last time we mopped south of 10th Street, Pang Rolin area, do you remember?

- The place where we met three girls bathing naked! Will we pass by that place again this time, Mr. Chien?- A boy who was not familiar with the topography of this area asked again.

- No, we're going north this time. This direction is very thorny. I know, just now there was a war at the 321 Ridge. You have to pay attention up there when going tomorrow!

When approaching the area of 321 Ridge, the whole squad formed a vertical line, people were from 5 to 7 meters away from each other. At about ten o'clock at the foot of the mountain, they met a herd of wild boars, each of them was round, plumping meat. Some of them were fighting for something. The other animals also grabbed the intestines, pulled back and forth… Lacking food, craving a meal of wild boar, one person raised his gun to kill the fattest one, Chien approached and stopped:

- Do not shoot!...

- This place is far from the enemy, they can't detect us. Shoot one to revel. This is a wild boar, not a pig, Mr. Chien!

- It's not that I'm afraid the enemy can hear us. I also know this is not a pig of the people!...- Saying that, Chien's eyes blinked, his neck seemed to choke, whispering: "That's our brother!...".

- Why is the pig our brother? I don't understand what you said!...

Everyone came close to each other, the squad leader explained:

- These pigs are big and fat thanks to "eating" our people who stayed here when they attacked and captured 321 Ridge at the beginning of the last rainy season...

- !...!...

Hearing the sound, the pigs ran away into the forest. Chien's squad continued to search around the foot of the mountain. A boy in front of him discovered a nearly one-meter-long iguana with its snout tucked into the chest of a decaying skeleton. The iguana didn't pay attention, it was so fascinated with pulling the bait that only when a person came to push the butt of a gun into its tail did it come out, turn its head to look and then run away... Chien told his brothers to pick up the bones of the legs and arms and the skull of the skeleton to put in a bag. Looking at the skull with two deep eye sockets, worms crawling out, everyone panicked. But it was the remains of their comrades, they calmed down and brought them back to the regiment's morgue...

All that night, Chien's squad could not sleep. Whenever they took a nap, they saw skulls showing their teeth everywhere, rolling their eyes, following from behind and then going forward to catch up. A person was so scared, he squealed when sleeping, getting up from the hammock, grabbing the gun and hiding in the corner of the cellar... It took a whole week for Chien's squad to return to a normal state of mind.

Chapter 18

Nguyen Mong Hung looked up at Phearak for a few seconds and then turned his eyes to Chi Tai. He knew, they were asking him to talk specifically about their very loving Regiment Commander. But he wanted to talk about the Infantry Regiment of which Xuan Manh was the commander through the Regiment Commander. He continued:

... Regiment commander Ngo Xuan Manh squinted at the 20x30 enlarged black and white photo brought by the scout leader. A photo of the Regiment Command with the provincial delegation during the Chon Ch'nam Festival of Poetry in the Clouds at the courtyard of Pailin Pagoda.

- "It's him!" Xuan Manh pointed to a man in his thirties, with a bony face, deep eyes hidden under thick eyebrows which looked like two caterpillars, ears perked up like mouse ears in a Disney animation. He stood next to Xuan Manh, on his right was Nari, the leader of the delegation. Xuan Manh told the head of the reconnaissance department: "The other day at the Provincial Military Intelligence Department, I met and exploited him. It was this guy that Ta Mok planted in the provincial office to investigate important targets in Pailin. The targets that Ta Mok is in need of investigation, including our regiment headquarters and the 105mm artillery field. He took advantage of the last Tet holiday, accompanied by a provincial delegation to investigate by legal means. Damn it, the enemy standing next to you without you knowing it!"

Xuan Manh pulled the scout leader to a map of the combat area:

- He said, at this stream is the headquarters of Ta Mok. This man often drags all of them here to meet and discuss plans. They do not stay in one place, for fear of being ambushed. This is the permanent residence of Ta Mok! - Manh pointed to a low hill, sandwiched between two streams.

The scout leader moved his index finger along a shallow stream, his eyes shining as if he had just remembered something:

This is the headwaters of the Sang Ke River. This place once, the 2nd battalion sent a search force up there, was fired by mortar shells, we also suspected that there was an enemy base on the stream head. In this area, so far, no force has set foot there. It is possible that Ta Mok relied on the rugged terrain to serve as a logistics base and set up his headquarters!

Regiment commander Xuan Manh could not take his eyes off the high point with two contours.

- The prisoner said: This place has three wooden houses, roofed with green corrugated iron, mixed with the green color of the forest, so it is difficult to detect. Two houses are located on two stream branches, with two squads of soldiers guarding. As for the third house, near the confluence, it was dedicated to Ta Mok to live with Thai women!... He said: "Ta Mok is very cunning, we can't kill him. If you want to go to that place, you should follow this stream, going up from the bottom!"

Xuan Manh looked up at the reconnaissance leader:

- Is there any way to break in here?!- He often probed the abilities of his subordinates before assigning tasks. The reconnaissance director did not answer, he pondered for a long time. If only Mr. Mai was still here, it would be a piece of cake to get inside that place.

- Last time, Mr. Mai died in Parrot's Beak due to negligence on the way back. The other two escaped. How about we send these two to continue, they have experience anyway!

- I also think so. Towards the front, they are much more cautious, in addition to the scout force, they will surely spread mines. Breaking in from behind is the most unexpected!

- Ta Mok is a cunning old fox, getting into his place is not easy. How did our scouts recognize him? - The scout leader was confused. Breaking into that area is already difficult, destroying it is many times more difficult!... - The scout leader still hesitated. According to the other guy, Ta Mok had a recognizable feature that he had a broken leg and he staggered. He was wounded in the battle of a volunteer army unit at Ta

Sanh during the dry season of the previous year. And on this front, who knows about him?

Since that day, Xuan Manh could not sleep at night. The confluence of the stream with the corrugated iron house hovered in front of his eyes. Although he had not reached that place in the field, he only looked at the map, from the symbols of dry streams, water condensate, the flat and thin contours, the thick places around that high point as if they were in the palm of the regiment commander. Then Xuan Manh wondered: how to break into it? When you go there, how do you know he is Ta Mok? Knowing him and then how to eliminate him?... Mobilizing forces to accompany scouts cannot be secret to investigate, if the investigation is completed and then returns to lead troops, we will lose our chance, they might even know our intentions so they will move to another place, like a game of hide and seek, it won't do anything. There were many questions that have not yet been answered satisfactorily. It's past midnight. The guard soldier, still carrying his gun, walked past, back and forth, guarding the front yard. Xuan Manh took a flashlight and went to the chief of staff's house. He thought, "Thanh Multiflorous knotweed" often had sharp ideas, it was rare for a chief of staff who had both been through school and was rich in battle experience, he would probably have a way. When facing difficult and complicated situations, the person that Xuan Manh trusted the most was the Chief of Staff:

- You haven't slept yet, Thanh?!

- I am looking for the best route for scouts, so that it is close but safe and unexpected!

- I haven't been able to sleep since the evening because of what you just said!

- I think our scouts can go there anyway, but infantry cannot do so easily. This area is very rough! - Thinking for a moment, "Thanh Multiflorous knotweed" looked up at the regiment commander: "I planned a plan to attack this place!".

- Keep talking!

- If this is their base, there will definitely be a way from the other side of the border!

- Of course! As in base 321, from the line along the border line, there are branch lines that "pull over"!

- I will find a way from Thailand to this base!

- You mean...

- Let me finish. When attacking the target, we will let loose on the roads across the border. Just a force strong enough to directly attack their base!

- That's good! But the main thing is to find out where Ta Mok's base is, then find out their escape route when we attack!

Thanh thought differently:

- We can also do the opposite!

- You mean from the back road to track Ta Mok?

- Correct! This method can be easier than scouring the forest for them like finding a needle in a haystack! How many streams are on the map? There are junctions that are "condensers" that are not on the map!

When Xuan Manh saw that Thanh was right, he patted the chief of staff on the shoulder:

- I still don't get it wrong about you!

The scout leader was called up. So from then until morning, the three minds gathered, deciding on the plan outlined by Chief of Staff Thanh.

The reconnaissance group led by Mui went up to the ridge 505. Here was a squad of the 2nd battalion holding the post. Now they saw the value of this spending peg. Normally, it stood here as a watchtower, the presence of the soldier here to prove that Cambodia's sovereignty was complete right at this border marker, the volunteering soldiers stood side by side with Cambodian revolutionary armed forces, who were here day and night to guard the town of Pailin before the envious eyes of the enemy who wanted to return to the ruins. Today, this point was the springboard, the starting point for a new plan, the plan to attack Ta Mok's base in the mountains south of Pailin.

It was not too difficult to find, the reconnaissance team discovered a wide trail with ox cart tracks along the west side of the border.

- This road runs north and then turns to base 321! - A scout soldier said to Chief Mui.

- How do you know?

- The day before yesterday, Mai and I met this road in the upper section, only a few kilometers from here. This road will definitely go up there!

At night, the light of the moon was dim, as if they were walking in the fog. Headlights from Thailand's interior shot fan-shaped rays of light into the sky. The sound of a car rumbling from afar. Along the border between the two countries remained quiet and cold. The scout team followed the trail heading south.

- There is a crossroad in front of us Mr. Mui!...- The soldier in front stepped back and said to the leader.

Mui cautiously stepped up. A road turned eastward through the darkness. Then another road. From here going south, there may be more such trails. Mui stopped, determined the direction, and then the whole nest followed the path and entered the eastern forest and disappeared in the dark.

After more than two hours of groping and wriggling, the reconnaissance team encountered a shallow stream. In the dry season, the stream did not have a drop of water. Mui went first, leading the whole squad down the stream. Suddenly there was a very small noise up ahead, and then the smell of uncleanness wafted through the air, hitting the nose. The scouts followed the stream, lying with their ears on the ground. This was the experience to determine where the sound was coming from, far or near. Mui strained his eyes to see through the night. In the dim light of a house under a tree line, the house was lined with planks.

- You guys are on guard here, I'll crawl in to see. Notice the top of the stream. According to the news, their security forces are up there!...

- You can rest assured! This is the place in the deep forest. It's late, maybe they don't go out anymore!

The scout leader Mui crawled like a lizard, crawling through the mounds, rocks, and stumps to approach the house. Through the gap between the two pieces of plywood, the light of the Manchon lights inside shone out. A man was lying on his back between two women, they were naked, one was kissing on the man's rough face, Mui heard a slurping sound like she was sucking her lover's tongue. Hey, one was leaning on a wooden bed, face down in the other guy's crotch, doing the same thing as in the "dirty film" that once when he was at home Mui borrowed a sex tape to watch sneakily... A black "army ants" bravely marched across the Mui's feet, they discovered there was human sweat on those legs, so they gathered together to bite, Mui felt a sharp pain but did not dare to move, gritting his teeth to endure. Seeing no response from that leg, the ants called each other to continue marching.

Mui looked at the crack of the wooden wall, they were still licking, still sucking. It seemed that the foreplay was enough to move on to another phase, the most intense phase to reach the extreme pleasure of the sex game. One was sitting and watching, the other was leaning on her butt, her white butt was as white as gypsum, inviting, the other guy was thrusting from the back, thrusting from the bottom... Mui has to admit that son of a bitch was as strong as an old goat. Back at home, his aunt's goat herd in Ninh Thuan, there were hundreds of female goats, only one male goat was in charge. The other guy just "thrusted" until the woman watching could not bear it, jumped in to take turns. Mui was suffering from the disease of "spermatorrhea, wet dream" and malaria which caused him yellow eyes, yellow skin, yet lying in the dark observing their actions, Mui's crotch was wet before he became aware of it. The other one squealed like a pig when she was provoked. Mui was startled and the other guy also stood up and hobbled to the clothes hanger, going to the bathroom...

"That's exactly Ta Mok (!)", Mui recognized him from his staggered foot...

- I just saw Ta Mok with two sluts in that house! - Mui came back to tell the two soldiers on guard.

- What took you so long, Mui? How do you know Ta Mok is in there?

- That's right, I recognized him, because his legs were limping! - And why it took so long, Mui didn't say...

When breaking into here, the reconnaissance team only discovered a house, when coming back, there were houses in every direction, the big one, the small one, the corrugated iron roof, the thatched roof... It turned out that the scouting team approached along the dried stream while there were dozens of houses on both sides of the river... Overnight and the next morning, the reconnaissance team returned to checkpoint 505. The sun had just risen from the distant mountain, releasing brilliant rays of light down to Pailin valley to gradually dissolve the fog which looked like a curtain, opening up a very airy space. Along the way, birds chirping, dancing in the trees welcome the heroes from Ta Mok's lair back...

Chapter 19

Coming to this section, before continuing, Nguyen Mong Hung asked Chi Tai:

- Have you been to Da Nang city?

- He only asked Chi Tai personally, because he was a veteran of the Vietnam volunteer army. As for Phearak and his wife, he knew that they had never stepped foot in Da Nang. Chi Tai said:

- Yes. After withdrawing from the country, after a short time, I returned to Pailin with Phearak, so I have never been to Da Nang!

- I am asking to tell you, in Da Nang city, there is a street named Tran Duy Chien. Chien was a soldier of the Regiment commanded by Ngo Xuan Manh. There are many soldiers in this regiment who deserve to be awarded the title of Hero, but Tran Duy Chien has been favored to name a street in a major Vietnamese city. It is no coincidence, we should understand that: Tran Duy Chien is only the representative of a generation of young people born after the great victory in the spring of 1975, above all, the noble sacrifice for national service and the resurgence of Cambodia, I will talk about him in the following section. Mong Hung said:

...The battlefield had entered the rainy season. The rainy season that year, on the Pailin front, no one could forget. The rain poured down, the clouds covered the ruined town. The green forest carpet was swept by the wind, bobbing like waves chasing each other. Trees twisted and cracked, tangled, and broke. Lightning flashed like whips in the air, tearing the dark clouds into pieces. Water poured down from the hillsides to fill streams, turning roads into rivers, ponds and lakes into sea. The precarious bridges connecting the two banks were washed away by the flood downstream, leaving broken and muddy roads. 10th Street was cut into sections, and the town of Pailin was completely isolated.

Chien's squad wore raincoats, each leaning on a tree or termite mound in the middle of a deep forest. The raincoat was tattered, the water crept into the back, into the chest, down the two pant legs below the navel, the legs and arms were numb and aching, the teeth were chattering. The whole squad stood like that, leaning on the pistol grip, stroking their faces. The forest haemadipsa from under the rotten leaves, catching human breath, competed to find a target to attack. The dark yellow haemadipsa attacked from below, the green Haemadipsa from the bushes on both sides of the road quickly clinged to their backpacks and raincoats to break into people looking for hidden places, attacked above parts. When their stomachs were full of blood, they opened their mouths and fell to the ground, leaving fresh blood on their bodies, flowing endlessly. The soldier's blood mixed with rainwater, into rivers and streams, permeated the soil, and watered the trees. The pythons and snakes in the caves came out, making way for the water to swirl into the banks of the ravines and streams, they crawled up higher, looking for a place to avoid the flood. A Chinese green tree viper chose a Melicope ptelefolia, curled up a few times, raised his head, and waited. Chien discovered it, the two sides silently looked at each other, "If I don't touch you, don't touch me (!)", Chien looked up as if he was telling that.

The rain was still pouring, hundreds of thousands of cold, transparent raindrops shot down from above, tearing the leaves, breaking branches covering the paths. By noon, the sky was clear. The sun still peeked out from behind the dark clouds and looked down with its head as if to see if there was enough water in the valley after a dry season. It seemed that God saw that the bottom was full of water, the water was excessive, the dark clouds turned bright white, spread thin like a curtain and then rolled, wrapped around the top of the mountain like a mourning band on the head of the mother who was looking down sadly at her children under the ruined town of Pailin…

Seeing that the weather was clear, Chien's squad put a raincoat in his backpack, one of them crumpled a lump and stuffed it into a small pocket, his clothes were as wet as a drowned rat, his teeth were constantly clashing. On the long abandoned hillside trail, a group of black-clothed soldiers appeared in the distance in the thick clouds, they had discovered Chien's squad since the storm occured. The commander ordered all of them to secretly set the trap. An ambush field was quickly formed... The enemy team was about five or six people. They planted mines in front and on both sides in a V-shaped opening like a funnel, welcoming the enemy down from the north. The B40 guns, general-purpose machine gun, submachine gun pointed the barrel to the road surface ...

Unaware that he was going into a dangerous place, after putting his raincoat in his backpack, Chien ordered the whole squad to start, continuing along the dim road to the South. Every day, the units stood around Pailin town, they had to send their forces out to hunt down the enemy and protect the base. This was a measure to detect and prevent them remotely. The squad leader took the lead, the soldiers were five to seven meters away from the other, this distance was often applied so that if a mine exploded, it would reduce the number of casualties, or when encountering ambush from enemy infantry, it was also possible for someone to escape the first bullets. Nguyen Van Chinh, an ex-soldier who was the last of the squad, did the task of "locking the tail". The pouring rain just now, if there were any traces on the road, they would have been wiped away. The whole squad gradually entered the "funnel" like a ready-made gabion in front of them without even knowing they were entering the "death grave"...

Rain water remained on the leaves of the trees, and the wind blew and splashed the water. Lines of people walked in the rustling of forest leaves. Suddenly there was a deafening, head-splitting explosion right behind Tran Duy Chien. Next was the burst of AK guns interspersed with the rumble of B40 bullets. The whole squad was in the enemy's ambush. Chien hugged the gun, rolled around to the right to lean on a termite mound, this move Chien learned from Sergeant School of Mr."Grumpy" Thinh. In the back, Nguyen Thanh An and another person collapsed, lying motionless. Another soldier behind An was seriously injured and struggled with his broken leg. He was nearly ten meters away from the mine, so there was no problem, he quickly jumped over a big tree, leaning against it to pull a long series of bullets, the gun in his hand trembled. At the front, Chien responded promptly, a series of short bursts of bullets penetrating the groves in front and on both sides. A B40 flew from nowhere, hit the tree next to him, dozens of sharp and pointed bullet fragments pierced the body of the squad leader Tran Duy Chien...

The balance of power was not equal, the enemy was prepared, so they were in the initiative while Chien's squad was completely taken by surprise. The battle became more and more fierce. Only Chinh left, he fired two rounds of ammunition without knowing which direction the target was in, only hearing the crackling sound of AK bullets, the roar of B40 bullets, and 60 mortar shells surrounding them. Several times, Chinh rushed to the street, where Chien and his teammates were lying, but were all pinned down by the evil bullets. Teams of soldiers in black from the front and sides rushed out, shot more at the corpses, shot and disappeared into the forest...

In that critical situation, a force of allied units coordinated to sweep the southern area mobilized to provide support. But it was late. After the last rounds of bullets, the enemy withdrew from the battlefield. The squad was left with only Nguyen Van Chinh and an injured soldier... Oh! The fateful day, the day that ended the life of the volunteer soldiers at the end of the country of Pagodas. Chinh rushed to two bodies lying motionless in a pool of blood. Nguyen Thanh An lay face down on the mound, a bullet pierced from the left side of his chest to his back, the blood spurting out was frozen. Squad leader Tran Duy Chien was pinned by B40 shrapnel all over his body, he was lying on his side by the tree, the eyes of the son of the land of Quang were still wide open as death came to him too suddenly, they could not close, those eyes were still shining like pearls, looking up at the sky in the deep border... Chinh laid prostrate next to the dead comrades and dear fellow soldiers who had spent many days side by side, through thick and thin in the land full of traps. They sacrificed in their twenties on the Pailin front that were resounding with gunfire when the Cambodian battlefield had not yet come to an end.

After that traumatic incident, Chien and those who died were immediately taken to the ruined town of Pailin. As the condition of the battlefield did not allow, friends and comrades from the posts could only take turns to burn incense for the ill-fated. Standing in front of the deceased's bodies, Nguyen Van Chinh on behalf of the brothers that day, movingly said with tears in his eyes:

- Us, the lucky ones who are still alive, will continue your cause, even if we have to fight to our last breath on this land to avenge you. Then, we will bring you back to the motherland at all costs, that day will certainly not be far away. Goodbye!...

At this point, Nguyen Mong Hung told Chi Tai and Phearak that: "Tran Duy Chien left, leaving behind a bloody and tearful diary. If you have a chance, please read and remember about a time when Vietnamese volunteers fought in Pailin in the bloody time and in the country of pagodas, which made Cambodia what it is today.

Chapter 20

Determined to destroy the butcher Ta Mok, despite knowing this was not easy, Regiment Commander Ngo Xuan Manh mobilized enough forces to block all the paths across the border. He told Chief of Staff Thanh and head of reconnaissance:

- I will implement the strategy of "Shaking net for fish jumping"! How do you guys see?

"Thanh Multiflorous knotweed" laughed, a smile that carried many meanings:

- In the past, the Americans applied the tactic of "Using the net to throw the javelin", then "Phoenix catching bait"... to attack the Viet Cong. Now, our regiment commander has the initiative to use the tactic of "Shaking net for fish jumping" to attack the remnants of Pol Pot. Thus, the regimental commander's tactics seem to be similar to the American "using the net to throw javelin" strategy!...

- Only the nature is different, so the order of steps must be changed! - Xuan Manh said as soon as the Chief of Staff Thanh had not finished his words as if it was an opinion, before he spoke he was prepared to explain to the listeners every aspect. Americans "use the net" first and then "launch the javelin", and here will do the opposite or at the same time. Before, in the period of half-guerrilla, half-formal, we were not strong enough, we had to fight at night and rest during the day! Now, we have enough strength, and the enemy is the remnants, fighting in a guerilla style! Do you know the "legendary" saying of someone in the early stages of the border war: "Pot attacks us like how we attacked America in the old days, now we fight Pot like America fights us?". Almost exactly that!...

The Chief of Staff still refused, he wanted to argue with Xuan Manh so that the regiment commander could explain more for everyone to understand. Here, apart from the regiment commander and the Chief of Staff, there were not many people in the generation before the year of 1975. "Thanh Multiflorous knotweed" looked up and smiled at the regimental commander and said as if for everyone to hear:

-      In the military dictionary, I don't see a tactic called "Shaking net for fish jumping". Maybe, sometimes the city Police newspaper uses this phrase! But the fight against crime in the Police branch is different from our military!...

Xuan Manh knew that the Chief of Staff was just joking, his character was always like that, "Thanh Multiflorous knotweed" was smart enough to understand the main content of this fighting style. Xuan Manh also liked the seriocomic character of the Chief of Staff. Through such debates, it would make people understand more deeply about the nature, tactical characteristics and tasks of each force in the battle. "Thanh Multiflorous knotweed" was excited because his proposal the day before was accepted by the regiment commander, today it was discussed and applied. However, Xuan Manh still carefully explained the main contents of this way of fighting, because he understood that the victory or defeat of today's battle was not only in the mind of the highest commander here, which were the regiment commander and the regiment chief of staff but also was a combination of many factors, the efforts of all forces and each soldier. It's no exaggeration, even when the political commissar Binh was here, the main responsibility still belonged to him and the chief of staff Thanh:

- We will do the opposite of the prisoner's idea, that day he said that if he wanted to attack Ta Mok's place, we should break in from the East, follow the stream, his words were reasonable, because he knew the force that protected Ta Mok was in the west, there were only mines in the east. But how he can understand us, we will organize many groups, teams, compactly equipped, mainly directional mines, Claymore mines, breaking in from the West, blocking all roads across the border with ambushes, and catching them loose. Use a strong enough force to approach from the East, under the support of 105 mm cannon and infantry fire with high density and accuracy. Sudden attack from the front while the forces encircled, catching them behind still secretly, Ta Mok will have a hard time escaping!...

That night, the encirclement force was brought up to gather on the southern flank of 505 Ridge. They had not fought yet every soldier was as excited as the returning winner of the battle. Maybe they saw victory as being within reach. That night it was as dark as a blindfold, and each man found a piece of rotten wood with phosphorus on the back of the hat of the person in front of them, a long line, undulating and flickering like fireflies carrying lights. Chief of Staff Thanh still remembered, when he was fighting against the US, he was an information soldier who used to carry a backpack full of banana peels, walk in front of the formation, put a 30 centimeters long banana sheath, which was as wide as three fingers put together, every few steps. From behind, infantry followed the banana sheath to approach the target. It had been nearly ten years, but Thanh still remembered that initiative. Today he was the chief of staff of the regiment, applying this method to the troops to reach the target, but by attaching a piece of phosphorus to the back of each person's hat, this was the jungle, he could not use banana sheaths like in the plains. The border was quiet at night, the sound of dry branches being trampled by human feet was heard, sometimes the mice chasing each other gibbering. The group silently, quietly crossed the slope, waded through the stream and traveled through the forest to the South.

The first team discovered the crossroads. Here it was (!), the first crossroads that Mui's scouting team came to the day before, from there they followed a path to approach Ta Mok's house. Regiment commander

Xuan Manh instructed people to "deploy" a team there. The rest continued to head south, and deploy a team when reaching a trail. Just like that, the encirclement behind their backs became tighter and tighter. These teams were very carefully instructed that as the main target had not opened fire, they must keep absolute secrecy. If the enemy came from Thailand, just let them in. When we attacked Ta Mok base, we mainly eliminated the enemy from the East running through Thailand.

At the command post, regiment commander Xuan Manh and the head of the reconnaissance watched the penetrating force's every move. Perhaps these were the most stressful moments for those on duty tonight. From the day they set foot on the Pailin front, this battle of the 3rd Regiment was a special battle, especially because the fighting style was not recorded in any books, it was applied in practice in the battlefield with the weirdest object in history. Everyone held their breath until the front informed the entire force of deep penetration, the rear encirclement was deployed, ensuring secrecy and safety. Xuan Manh sometimes reminded the Chief of Staff to stick to the front. The regimental combat assistant marked on the map each step of the development of the two forces in two directions: the direction of encirclement, the direction of loose pick-up and the direction of frontal attack on the target, below the arrows there was time written and said:

- Hung "black" reports there were too many mines. The formation was about five hundred meters from the target!

- Remind him to hurry. Morning is coming! The direction of the Hung "black" is not crucial, but forces it to fire first!

- I understand!

- If it's late... - Xuan Manh said here, the information officer reported:

- There is a message from Hung, reporting that two gunners stepped on a mine and died on the spot!...

- I knew it, they would plant mines in the front, shift the main force to encircle the rear!... - Chief of Staff Thanh was satisfied with his proposal, which he considered very accurate. In life, no matter how small or big, if successful, it would give us excitement and a source of encouragement to commit. Thanh's opinion from the very beginning was accepted by the regiment commander. The frontal direction of Hung "black" was facing a bad situation, Thanh said:

- Necessity is the mother of invention, so it adds an element of surprise to the rear encirclement! But watch out, "The fish will jump if the date palm is shaken", but it doesn't jump into the "baskets" that are already arranged in the back but jumps somewhere else, it's a problem!...

Thanh was right, when the shells and mortars pounded around the confluence, where Ta Mok was holding two girlfriends a few days ago, the houses were shattered, people could clearly hear the screams of some sluts, mixed in with the roar of firepower bullets. Ta Mok's guards did not have time to bring weapons, the area was scattered in the forest ...

- Why didn't we hear rear encirclement force open fire? Call the 2nd Battalion! - Xuan Manh impatiently reminded the Chief of Staff.

- Maybe they haven't run far yet. "Have you heard people say "A drop in the ocean"?... I thought: maybe because they were surprised they ran out, they'll come back in a while!

Another good idea! Xuan Manh immediately thought of the evil trick of the bastard Ta Mok "the enemy advances, we move back, the enemy stops, we disturb". He ordered Hung "black":

- After capturing the target, quickly expand the search range, in case they ambush!

Hung "black" had mastered the target, panting and reporting to the regimental commander via 2w:

- A woman and two men died on the spot. They left behind three submachine guns and a communicator!

Hung "black" was very excited. Last time he was lost for seven days. Today there were scouts leading the way, otherwise it was difficult to reach the target as intended. Hung fought bravely, but when it came to the map and location he was very bad, he could be lost only by being a few kilometers out of the stationed area. It was not known who gave him the name Hung "black". His appearance was not so black, his face was delicate, his figure was tall, his temper was strong, when talking to someone, he kept looking straight at that person's face. Perhaps due to the rain and the sun and malaria, his skin was so pale, no one could be whiter when working in this area. As for the time he was lost the previous day, it could be due to encountering the enemy, having to wriggle and avoid in the complex terrain in the mountainous area, so it was difficult to avoid getting lost. Having lived here for nearly ten years, climbing many hills, wading many streams, not only Pailin but almost the whole length along the western border of Battambang province was in the palm of one's hand, many soldiers can get lost. Excited from killing a few enemies, obtaining a few guns, they did not quickly expand the range of mastery as instructed by the regiment commander, but huddled together. They started to counterattack. From the two sides of the hill, all kinds of rainbow firepower, direct fire quickly launched bullets, bullets were thick at the confluence, where Ta Mok's house was located; thick smoke, fallen trees, chaotic explosions, burning houses... Hung leaned his back against the stream to avoid bullets, reporting to the headquarters:

- We have captured the target, but are under fire from them. Request artillery reinforcements urgently!...

- If you ask for that, who can help you! An artillery is not like a rifle. Artillery must have targets and coordinates. In the immediate future, tell him to just use the firepower to fight back!... - The artillery assistant grumbled.

- Our firepower is out of ammo. Enemies are crowded!...

Without leaving the map, Xuan Manh stood up and sat down again, his heart was like a burning fire, he was surrounded by the chief of staff, chief of operations, chief of reconnaissance, chief of artillery, chief of engineer, chief information duty... On the faces that had been up all night, looked haggard, emaciated, shaggy hair, wispy beards, smelly clothes... people expressed anxiety when they learned that the battle where Hung "black" was in was coming to a drastic and unequal point.

Xuan Manh thought to himself: "Hung poked the hornet's nest (!)" and looked up at the officers sitting around as if asking them: what should we do (?). He remained calm and showed himself as a capable commander in all situations. Normally, when seeing his face it was taciturn, he rarely opened his mouth while arguing about something, he just listened. Especially since there were conflicts with Binh in commanding and directing, and then the "scandals" in the rear made his face even more taciturn. But in the silent moments where the battle before the situation unfolded was when he was kneading in the military thinking, looking for an optimal solution to win while minimizing the sacrifice of the teammates. Since the day Secretary Binh left the Pailin front, Uncle Tuyen had not returned from school, Xuan Manh had to shoulder the burden, both as regiment commander and as secretary, causing his face to be crumpled, his cheekbones became higher, his eyes sockets sunken into two black holes, his hair more silvery. Many times he thought: maybe that's better, all issues he can decide without any resistance from within. Gladly, there was a team of cadres who have been tested in the process of facing so many difficulties in this land, who were a reliable support for him, especially Chief of Staff Nguyen Van Thanh, "Thanh Multiflorous knotweed" and the directors were very congenial. Sitting around him, they were also worried, looking at the regimental commander.

- Hung reported this, what do you guys think?

The artillery assistant scratched his head:

- With that request, how can artillery be fired?

Next, each person said one sentence:

- Probably they were drunk with victory and then clustered together, became unwary, caught off guard and let the enemy turn the game around!

- Calling for artillery support whenever having trouble has become his habit, just let him handle it!

Everyone was talking about it, when the informer 2wat held a telegram, the chief of staff quickly grabbed it, signed it and read it to everyone: "The 2nd Battalion met the enemy, killed 5 guys, collected 5 guns. We're safe"!

- Ask again, is the enemy from the inside or outside? Check the characteristics of the corpses!... - Xuan Manh wanted to know if the number of enemies destroyed by the 2nd Battalion was from where Mr. Hung ran out or from across the border, and among those corpses was there Ta Mok or not?

- The 2nd Battalion killed the enemy but didn't hear the gunfire? - An assistant who was from Khu Tu asked.

- That direction is far and hidden from the mountains, how can they hear it!

There was a voice outside saying:

- Yes, I can't hear the sound of small guns, but I can hear mines exploding!

The explosion of mortar shells at the place of Hung "black" also gradually faded and then stopped completely. Hung reported to the headquarters:

- We have defeated the enemy's counterattack, and we are organizing to destroy the entire base area. Some more corpses were discovered!...

- Do you check the characteristics of those corpses to see if there is Ta Mok? - The regiment commander was still paying special attention to this notorious name.

- If he's dead, only DNA analysis will know! As for depending on the staggering foot, while no one knows what his face looks like, only God knows!... - "Thanh

Multiflorous knotweed" deduced. The artillery chief said:

- "Mr. Hung" kept calling for reinforcements, but he wouldn't cross his arms. I know!

Xuan Manh sat in front of the map to watch the progress of the raid on Ta Mok's lair from last night until now, the battle was reduced on it.

- This is a base located close to the border on difficult terrain. Since the collapse of the genocide regime, almost none of our forces and allied force have set foot here, so they are somewhat subjective. The approaching process of our troops, especially the encircling force from the rear, was kept a secret from beginning to end. The case of casualties in the advancing direction of the 1st Battalion led by Mr. Hung was a common occurrence on this front, it is known but difficult to avoid. So the battle carries a high element of surprise. While the enemy counter-attacked fiercely to push back our raiding forces in the front, the battles of the 2nd Battalion from the rear, although small in scale, directly threatened the morale of the enemy soldiers, forcing them to flee!...- Xuan Manh's above comment has partly shown the commanding ability of a regiment commander experienced with battle.

The battle was a victory, what remained in the mind of regiment commander Ngo Xuan Manh now was where the whereabouts of boss Ta Mok was? One hundred Pol Pot soldiers' lives were not equal to him alone...

Chapter 21

The attack on the enemy base at high point 321 by a volunteer force had just failed. Ta Mok has strengthened the force and the level of fortification was also more solid. Despite causing considerable damage to the enemy, after the fall of Com Rieng and Sala Krau, Ta Mok began to worry. He thought that this dangerous ridge would eventually fall into the hands of the Vietnamese army. If they could stand on it, what he had built along this border would be destroyed. He needed a method that did not require his men to be there, but the enemy won't be safe (!). Ta Mok's purpose was to maintain a transport corridor, penetrate inland, and not be intercepted by the enemy. Corridors were crucial to the survival of his exiled government. I did not need a high score, holding a high score only became bait for their artillery. Last month, when they attacked the Central Office base, I almost died in Cao Me Lai. That day, if I had not been fast, I would have been buried there by shells (!).

The rainy season ended, the last rains seemed to try to drain all the water left in the dark clouds, making them gradually melt, opening the door, revealing a vast and airy sky. The reconnaissance team cautiously crept through a thicket of thorny bamboo, aiming for the approaching high point 321. Less than a hundred meters from the foot of the mountain to the hillside, nearly a dozen landmines have been removed. The leader of the reconnaissance group saw that the division's deputy chief of staff Tong Xuan Lai seemed impatient, he stopped to explain:

- Too many mines, boss!

- Be careful! Beware of landmines. It's okay to be slow, there's no need to rush, life safety comes first!...- Lai said to reassure the scouts. Doing this job is like driving a car on a busy street, you can't be hasty, at the intersection, the red light has to stop, the person who is crouched in front of the car can't go fast. Previously, although he was a political officer, Tong Xuan Lai was "gifted" in the military, so he was "forced" to work as a consultant and now he is the Deputy Chief of Staff of the Division who was dispatched to the 3rd Regiment. On the first day he arrived at Com Rieng, he discovered a "strange landmine", a landmine brought back by a scout soldier. This "rotten mine" had a different size than the K58 and KP2 that soldiers often encountered. The reconnaissance company leader brought the mine to the staff office and asked the Chief of Engineers to instruct how to remove it. This guy thought: being the Chief of Engineers, he must know the types of mines and explosives. The Chief of Engineers took a look at the mine, looked around, above and below for a while, then shook his head. Politician Tong Xuan Lai held the mine up to eye level, examined the top and bottom to find out where the label and the detonator were. Can't see anything but the cylindrical body and the "snail colored" paint. Lai took the mine to a fortification about a meter deep, and dropped it from a distance.

- It won't explode, we'll find a way!

Of course, the landmine was still as mute as a fish.

- That's the first step!- Lai explained: "If it explodes, it will erase the secret in its heart. Now we still have the opportunity to discover what its belly contains. Maybe one of the reasons why so many soldiers lost their lives recently is because of this "strange mine" (!). Once, regiment commander Xuan Manh questioned this.

The work of "dissecting the strange landmine" was started. Many sleepless nights, constantly thinking about mines, Lai was determined to discover this type of mine to reduce casualties for the unit. He said:

- It is necessary to confirm one thing that whoever created it will know how to master it. Nothing is impossible. We don't make it, so now we have to find a way to treat it, that is, the secrets of its inventor and producer!

During the afternoon, while everyone was resting, Lai took out the landmine, found a quiet place, sat down and opened it. It took him an hour to take off the outer shirt, he discovered that inside the mine was very complicated with a "dry battery", short-circuited by a "ball" on a falling stake connecting the two terminals of the battery. Lai's eyes lit up and glittered, the wrinkles on his forehead deepened and dilated with a smile on his face, making his face radiant... Lai put the landmine down in front of him, wiped his hands with dirt on both sides of his butt and opened the chest pocket of the military shirt he was wearing to take out a pack of Samit cigarettes, pulled out a cigarette, lit it in his mouth, "rewarding himself" for successfully uncovering the secret of the evil and malicious murder technology of the enemy...

The battalion politician called the scouts to explain the exploding principle of the "strange mine" and concluded why this mine did not explode:

-Firstly, the detonator was rotten due to the manufacturer's poor technique of moisture control (Lai's left hand held the mine body in front of him, the index finger of his right hand pointed at the detonator number 1, which was smaller than the tip of the chopstick). Detonator 1 often has problems. The second is because the power is out, while the fuse is still good, the fuse will not explode! This is a foreign-made anti-detection mine. However, I don't understand why they don't print labels on mines!

From that judgment, Lai started experimenting by changing the detonator, replacing the battery. But right now, on the battlefield, you couldn't get these things. Detonators were available, run to the Chief of Engineers to ask, if you don't have the 1st detonator, you can use the 4th detonator. As for the battery, where to find a tiny dry battery to attach to the landmine.

Tong Xuan Lai refused to stop there, the main purpose of discovering the secret of the landmine was to master it, to force it to submit to our will. Lai continued to experiment by having a "middle battery" fighter outside the mine, because he thought he was researching to know the explosive principle of the mine to neutralize it, not researching to produce it, so it was not necessary to put the battery in the mine - Only the "marble" when falling that caused short-circuiting was the most important detail of that "strange mine".

Seeing that it was certain, believable, Lai first brought the mine to a fortification, put it down there, and put the battery on the bank to connect the last for safety. Xuan Lai looked at the scout soldiers sitting around:

- Get out and find a place to hide!

Lai was lying on the ground, holding a stick from above, poking down. There was a loud "bang" sound, ringing in both ears, rock and soil jumped up and fell down the fence. The squirrel and his wife were in love on the top of a nearby tree, startled, jumping around looking for a place to hide. Agencies and units alert everyone to carry guns to battle positions. When they were all down in the trenches, guns were drawn in a ready-to-battle position, until they looked up to see Tong Xuan Lai standing there, grinning, his face looked like a guilty person... At that time, everyone was relieved. Fortunately, Lai only suffered minor injuries to his arm from holding the stick down.

Through this experiment, Politician Tong Xuan Lai concluded: "When encountering this type of mine, it is best to detonate it, not remove it!...". Today, around the high point of 321 does not rule out that they can also use this type of mine to kill the opponent.

Tong Xuan Lai walked behind the reconnaissance team, carrying a Canon camera. Not a war correspondent, but in his backpack there was always a camera with Kodak film pre-installed and a pair of brand new batteries, ready to capture what he loves on the march, in the middle of the bomb and bullets and even revels and parties of soldiers. In the album he brought to the international battlefield, people discovered many valuable and topical documents: the corpses of Pol Pot soldiers with bloated stomachs, landed by green flies lying on the trenches, in the forest at the base of Cao Me Lai, O Da, Com Rieng, the 130mm long barrel cannon that the Front distributed to the division that raised its barrel proudly at Nam Sap during the dry season campaign in 1982, the tanks and armored vehicles on the way to the border, the typical soldiers in the emulation movement returned to attend the "Congress to celebrate the merits" of the division, with squad leader Tran Duy Chien in it, and also the suspension bridges over the Sang Ke River, Mong Con Bo Ray River, several engineering soldiers perching above; The 3rd Regiment's letters and arts team was rehearsing performances to prepare for the festival under the majestic Pailin temple, imprinted on the deep blue sky with gold glitter glittering in the morning sun, the couples love each other in the Apsara dance in the land of Angkor and there were also pictures of the couple taken at his wedding in Ho Chi Minh City. The photos with Lai in them maybe he asked someone to take them for him, because the Canon camera had technical problems so it couldn't take pictures in automatic mode, it should have been "off policy" to be in "soldier's museum." This album, if any journalist can get it, there is a lot of material to find on the topic of war, especially the images of "Buddhist Army" in the country of pagodas and towers... Lai's purpose today was to record what's on this troublesome high point 321. What's up there that dozens of comrades have had to lie on since the dry season last year until now...

Forward, the reconnaissance team still persisted, quietly doing the dangerous thing, which may disintegrate after an explosion, but still have to do, which was to open a path from the foot of the mountain to the top, only half a meter wide yet they had to travel from the morning until midday to arrive at the place. At the same time, this time, they once again went to find the scout squad leader Mai, sacrificed last time, maybe the remains were somewhere in the Parrot's Beak area... Along the way, there were many mines. The green "snail" KP2, K58 mines were twisted by the scouts and scattered on both sides of the path. Why was it called K58 and KP2 (?). Many people thought that: the time when K58 mines were produced (probably from 5.8), the population of Cambodia was five million, eight hundred thousand people, and Pol Pot announced that he would fight Vietnam until the last Cambodian. As for KP2, someone said: after the successful "genocide", the Khmer Rouge only needed two million "pure" people to go to Socialism... Maybe. In addition to those deductions, only heaven knows what the labels of those "killer bombs" mean...

The reconnaissance team and the divisional deputy chief of staff reached the top a little after noon. The sun was set to the West. On a rough area less than fifty square yards, trees were broken by shrapnel, shriveled, and collapsed in a sprawl. The branches are stripped of leaves from the base to the tip. Rocks were as big as buffalo, black, broken, crushed. No fortifications, no trenches. The black crows, hovering in the middle of the overcast sky, landed on the bare branches, lowered their heads, and glanced. The bodies around the hillside, after a rainy season, rotted, smelled, which caused the crows to fly to.

Regiment commander Xuan Manh sent the company DKZ75 up, placed right on the high point of 321, two guns, pointed to the West. Song Xuan Lai looked at the recoilless cannon and then at the rocks in front of him. He struggled to find a position and an angle to capture some photos on this "historic" high point, a bold mark in the years of guarding Pailin, where dozens of soldiers died in the battle at the end of the dry season of the previous year. Lai crouched down, leaning his butt to the West to capture the front of the DKZ. The light was good. Behind the cannon is a natural "font", the cannon was clearly visible in the middle of the green forest, in the sky, there were white clouds floating in the wind. "This picture is going to be good(!)"-Lai thought and leaned back like a high-class photographer, lifting the lens a little higher. There was a terrifying explosion under his feet, rock and dust erupted like an overturned funnel, causing Lai to fall in front of the DKZ75, blood spurting out both legs of his pants, one leg was cut off to the knee, thrown a few meters away... Suddenly, Lai couldn't scream out loud, lying unconscious. The gunners ran over, gathering all the bandages to stop the fresh blood that was gushing out from the Deputy Chief of Staff's legs. He was immediately taken to the 3rd Regiment infirmary in the center of Pailin town. Tong Xuan Lai's job as "deputy photographer" had to "retire" from that day...

Chapter 22

Attending a conference at the United Nations, Ieng Sary hastily held a meeting with the government to report the important news that they had been waiting for so many years. However, this meeting was missing some key people: Prime Minister Pol Pot was at Anlong Veng, an important base inland, Nuon Chea and Khieu Samphan went to Ampe. Only the trio: the Secretary of State, the Secretary of Defense and the Chief of the General Staff remained at home, as the border front, which determined the existence of the exiled government, had no standing place yet. Therefore, where there was a hot spot, these three must be present. Their country's destiny now depended only on the diplomatic and defense fronts, which may turn the situation around. The front headquarters on the border front, where people often gathered for meetings, was destroyed by the enemy. That day, the Chief of the General Staff Ta Mok only managed to hug one woman to run away, while the other woman broke her skull right when the first barrage hit the base... Now at another location in the Ta Sanh area, the Government members in this key direction had arrived in full force. Everyone thought that this meeting should have been in the presence of Pol Pot, but he rarely met with members of the government. On the contrary, the members of this strange alliance also did not want to be with the prime minister to create more tension. Even his "comrades-in-arms" once said: "The prime minister is the most hated of the regime's abominable men!".

The diplomacy minister cheered, raising his voice full of confidence:

- We are moving towards a total solution to the Cambodia problem! Vietnam has agreed to withdraw its troops, but the time has not been set!... Before the opening of the United Nations General Assembly meeting, I had a private meeting with the advisor. He let me know in advance some of the content that will be discussed in the conference!...

The forward headquarters, after being destroyed by the Vietnamese army, was set up in another most discreet place, close to the border with Thailand. Although the government was meeting in a room guarded by soldiers inside and outside, when giving the news of the private meeting to the adviser, Ieng Sary lowered his voice, like there was a hand turning the volume a transistor radio that was screaming all over upside down to make the voice softer, so that some had to tilt their ears to the Foreign Minister to hear clearly: *"This time we will discuss some core issues, one is to set a time for the withdrawal of foreign troops from Cambodia, the other is to establish the "Supreme National Council (SNC)", accompanied by a United Nations monitoring mechanism. The adviser put one more condition, that from now on, in international forums, in documents, the phrase "genocide" must not be used!"*

When they heard this, some of them lowered their heads, like a child who knew his mistake in front of an adult. Maybe they thought that in the past, in their bloodlust, they were too strong-willed, causing the dead fields, the mounds of skulls with their teeth and eyes wide, collecting debts all over the country. If only I had been a little more lenient during my years in power..., but now it's too late. Like a giant water bug who was spicy even when being near death, Ta Mok said:

- So Vietnam has admitted defeat in Cambodia, so they agreed to withdraw its troops, otherwise it won't be long before they release the lucrative bait that has cost hundreds of thousands of lives in this country! This also shows that our struggle on the diplomatic front has been won, the international community still supports us!...

The whole meeting room moved, not only the three key members but also many "sycophants" of nearly a third of the government that were often snakes in the grass; everyone wanted to talk, wanted to argue, but didn't know where to start. The secrets that have not yet come out are lying in the bald head of the minister. Seeing Ieng Sary open his mouth to continue speaking, all those present in the meeting room were silent and listened. The mentality of the person standing on the podium, seeing the crowd below attentively, eyes kept looking at the mouth of the person who was speaking as a gift for the presenter. Ieng Sary, as he was encouraged, the more confident he became, the more energetic he said:

- China is indeed a farsighted person, their voice is persuasive, forcing Vietnam to accept the conditions set by them.!... The world situation is having favorable developments for us, we need to seize the approaching opportunity!...

Chief of the General Staff Ta Mok sat next to Son Sen, he immediately thought of the opportunity that Ieng Sary had mentioned a few years ago, that: the recapture of Pailin during the transition between the withdrawal of Vietnamese troops and the taking over of Hun Sen's army. He sneered: "That guy is so smart. What a trick of a saliva business man (!). Ing Sary cited two events that created the opportunity for his fallen government, like a drowning man, struggling in a whirlpool, glimpsed a rotten log ahead: One is the Socialist countries in East-Europe and the Soviet Union are in danger of collapse, Vietnam will lose supplies from the Soviet Union while having just ended the war with the Americans, the economy is exhausted again so when pursuing this war, how long it will last, it's right for them to withdraw. If only they withdrew their troops earlier, would it be beneficial for both sides (?). Second, if Vietnam wants to keep the socialist regime, it must cling to China, a large socialist country, mountains and mountains, rivers and rivers. Vietnam wants to normalize relations with China more than ever… and China is our benefactor. They sacrificed tens of thousands of people on the northern border front of Vietnam also for us, sharing the burden with us in this war. These are very beneficial events, very delicate, allowing us to have absolute confidence in the solution to come!...

Almost in the media from then on, no one mentioned the word "genocide" that was about to be put on the conference table. Not using "genocide", what word to use to match the more than two million Cambodians murdered. Those of you sitting here, no matter how unintelligent, understand that: China put this content on the agenda on purpose. They knew the inevitable outcome of the war in advance, so it was better to prepare for the post-war period right now... This word only had "one word", but it was related to the background and career of the people sitting here after the war was over. They paved the way for the steps that followed decades later. If this was the case, you could regain the government, it's okay, maybe you still have many forces that supported you, on the other hand, if you failed, how could you avoid the international criminal court of The Hague. It was true that China was farsighted, they had devoted a whole chapter, demanding the eradication of the word "genocide" in order to erase a criminal record...

- We need to urgently prepare for the "post-war plan" when the time will come soon! - Ieng Sary has long thought of jumping into the town of "future capital" of the exiled government: When he jumps into it, where will his members of government be located in this ruined, devastated town when there is not a single house left intact. He thought further: how to establish a relationship with Hun Sen's government, what kind of regime for a country that has been destroyed by people like him during his years of ruling the country with axes and bayonets, pistol grip. As a Minister of Foreign Affairs, Ieng Sary did not forget to immediately think of the neighboring countries that had cooperated with his government in times of need, and also the dream of the fertile lands in the Southwest of Vietnam... without even thinking about being in the docks of an international court? As for the "sycophants" sitting here, when they heard the Foreign Minister's announcement, they were overjoyed. In the immediate future, they didn't need to know what the future will be, there's nothing left to gain (!), they just wanted to quickly end all these years of hiding in this forest, that mountain, the future was dark, the family was separated, scattered everywhere...

Chapter 23

A beautiful day in the border area. In the morning, the warm sunlight from the east shines down on the tiled roof of the majestic and fanciful temple, brightening up the iridescent gold layer that has been covered by time for decades. On the front yards of the houses, only the walls of the house were left with jagged walls, sparkling with blue, red, purple and yellow colors of precious stones mixed with sand and gravel. Flocks of parrots with light blue feathers flew back from everywhere, circled and landed on the scattered peach branches left in the ruined neighborhood. Everything here seems to have woken up earlier than usual.

At the 3rd Regiment, many brothers burst into tears like children when they heard the news from nowhere that the Vietnamese Volunteers were about to return home.

Oh! Dream or reality. Under the units, many people did not believe, on the front posts, despite the death god lurking on the road, there was a soldier who crossed the forest, crossed the stream, and asked Ngo Xuan Manh:

- Is it true, Chief?

- What do you mean "is it true"?!... Xuan Manh was also excited, looking up and pretending not to understand.

- I heard that we are about to withdraw our troops back home!

- About to withdraw, but not already!

- We were thrilled to hear the news!...

I don't know where this news came from, a few years ago people also heard it twice, maybe they dreamed? This time it spread quickly through the Regiment like a thunderstorm in the middle of a dry season, like a stream of warmth blowing from the plains to dispel the cold on the frontier during the long nights of standing guard, and as if swimming in the floodwaters, After all, the strength was exhausted, looking ahead, there was a float on a small island... Nguyen Van Chinh and Ho Ngoc and the brothers of the 5th company immediately thought of the oath they took before when Tran Duy Chien was a battalion commander: "Whoever is still alive must bring the remains of the dead back to their hometown (!)"... The boys discussed: "We will stay to do this if requested by the leader!".

Regiment commander Xuan Manh did not show it on the outside like his soldiers, because he was cautious when he did not really believe that he would be able to voluntarily withdraw his troops back to the country, he was always like that, but he felt worried, he kept going into the house and then going out into the yard again, his hands do not know what to do at this time, he answered ambivalently:

- You tremble when you just heard about the news, what if we really withdraw, so what?

- But we see that the enemy is still around this town, if we withdraw today, tomorrow this place will fall right into their hands! Maybe on the way back to the country, it will be difficult to come back!...

Inwardly, Xuan Manh also felt worried, not very secure when the danger of losing this ruined town was waiting. What will happen after they left here and handed it over to the 196th Division while the new Cambodian state is revived. Very possible. It's not just Xuan Manh and the soldiers of the 3rd Regiment who were looking forward to this event every day, but on this front and across the country as well, thousands of officers and thousands of volunteers all shared the same mood that it was time to hand over the management of this country to the Cambodian people, but they still did not feel secure at all. The regimental commander was even more pleased and proud of the soldiers who have stood on this front for ten years now! Nine years of long resistance war to win half of Vietnam. Ten years of fighting with the Americans, the country was merged. More than ten years of doing international missions to help the Cambodian people escape the genocide, rebuild the government from the number "zero". While the homeland and the country are peaceful, so many people have to die at the end of the country, those who are still alive are full of illnesses and injuries, their youth has passed over the years. However, in the atmosphere of the days of preparing to leave the battlefield and return to the rear, there were still officers and soldiers who were still worried about the future of this neighboring country, whether it would survive or fall into the hands of the enemies again when Ta Mok and his whole team were still there, just around here, they were waiting for an opportunity to jump in... Withdrawing troops back to the country, it's clear that the joy was obvious, who did not shed the tears of joy at the news were no different than in the glorious hour of April 30, 1975 when the South was completely liberated. And how great, how noble was the worry of the soldier today, how noble when he realized that each person here was so small compared to what ten years later has brought to this country, and above all for the traditional solidarity between the two peoples of Vietnam - Cambodia has been restored. Did the years on this mortal land mold the soldiers of the 3rd Regiment to have a firm bravery, a resilient will, steadfast loyalty, and purity of a generation for a time and forever...

One of the things to do before the official order to withdraw troops was that the units remove all the remains of martyrs at temporary cemeteries across the front to return home. The cemetery next to Battambang airport was several hectares wide, every month someone died and was brought here for burial. Over ten years, thousands of martyrs were transported to the rear by cars and planes. The graves were covered with grass, interspersed with the bright red earth graves, aligned, straight, horizontal, vertical, evenly spaced like a squad preparing for a parade. There was a time when there were many martyrs, the burial team just picked up this person to move, and immediately brought another person down. Tran Duy Chien's grave along with Tho, Phuong, Lam "deaf", Dai Bang and some brothers from the same company, although the time of their sacrifice was different, yet without plan, they were gathered here in an area so that in the other side, they could be accompanied...

Today was the final relocation of the remains of martyrs taking place at the cemetery next to Battambang airport. Representatives of agencies, departments, mass organizations and commanders of volunteer forces were present very early to see off the outstanding children of the Vietnamese people back home. A long line of hundreds of small earthenware was waiting to excavate the graves and put the remains in. The most miserable, the most terrifying were the newly buried graves, the meat had not yet melted into the ground, the unloading team must use a knife to cut along the bones, separate the meat and then pump water to wash the bones. Sometimes they had to spray perfume on their masks, but sometimes they couldn't stand the stench that sticks to their guts and throws up. The stench from the dead bodies just rose, causing the crows to fly everywhere, more and more, they hovered in the air for a while and then swooped down, circling around the people as if they were used to this scene before, waited for the opportunity to rush in to rob the pieces of meat that people have not been able to fill, if were were not careful, they may even steal the skeletons...

Martyr Tran Duy Chien was brought up from the grave. The captain opened the blue plastic sheet and saw that there was something on the remains of the son of Quang that was not like other martyrs. According to soldier Nguyen Van Chinh, Chien died in the enemy ambush that year because he was shot by a B40 bullet from a distance, hit a tree, and many fragments of bullets pierced his body. But when excavated, put the remains into the small crockery, people saw a few AK bullets falling, the skull part was no longer intact, broken into many pieces. Most likely, the barbarian enemy, before fleeing, fired more shots, causing his body to deform... The captain of the loading and unloading team was about to keep some bullets, and he didn't think it was for any purpose other than the mood of a soldier who wanted to keep something related to the decades-long war that he was lucky to be alive today. But then he stopped, then put those bullets in the remains, packed and shipped back to the country...

On the way to the cemetery, the delegates stood on both sides, one side was the representative of the army units, the other side was the locality, holding the flags of the two countries and fresh bouquets of flowers. Before putting the remains in the car, the regiment commander Ngo Xuan Manh, on behalf of the volunteer army unit, went along the formation to greet the local representative, suddenly he met Nari, now

Vice President and President of the Provincial Women's Union. Today she wore a traditional outfit, a sarong printed with crimson flowers, an open-collared, tight-fitting white shirt that revealed a patch of white skin, her breasts were still full and sexy. However, this time, Nari looks "thinner", her facial skin was tighter. Perhaps life at the office was leisurely and materially enough to make her much younger and more beautiful than before. Unexpectedly, after the "memory of a lifetime" with her, that Xuan Manh assumed due to the unbridled male instinct, he was guilty of his wife and children. Previously, every time he went back for a meeting, Xuan Manh often visited Nari's mother and daughter, considering this as a place to return to during the years of international duty. These days, because of his job, he had not had the opportunity to return to the town, in his heart Xuan Manh wanted to have the opportunity to meet her again, but also wanted to rely on a certain reason not to repeat that inadvisable thing. Honestly, since that time, the image of Nari and the image of his wife and children kept interweaving in the mind of the regiment commander. Today, seeing Nari here again, both of them were confused and speechless. Nari's eyes filled with tears. Xuan Manh squeezed her hands tightly, but then they said a few words from the bottom of their hearts:

-       On behalf of the unit and on behalf of the individual, I would like to thank the people of Cambodia, thank the people of the province, thank Nari for wholeheartedly helping us to complete the task, this sentiment we will never forget!...

- It is the people of Cambodia, the people of Battambang province and me personally who must thank the Vietnamese soldiers. The State of Vietnam and Vietnamese volunteers are benefactors who saved the Cambodian people from genocide. Your great sacrifice, we and the Cambodian people will never forget!

Standing by Nari's side and holding her hand for too long was inconvenient, Xuan Manh went to the small crockery containing the remains of martyrs covered with the Vietnamese national flag and together with Nari raised their hands to the car. Two pairs of eyes met like lightning...

Chapter 24

On this trip back to the old battlefield this time, the old soldier Nguyen Mong Hung stayed for an extra day, it was not a waste of time and money. Knowing what happened after the withdrawal of troops back home that Chi Tai and Phearak told, Mong Hung did not expect that the relationship between Ngo Xuan Manh and the woman in the past made him remember all about what the regiment commanded by Regiment Commander Xuan Manh brought to the people in that border area. The great cause of Vietnamese volunteers in general and of this Regiment in particular was undeniably stopping the hands of the bloodthirsty people of a genocidal regime, saving the Cambodian people from extinction, and above all avoiding danger to neighboring countries. Who can be sure that, if they subdue Vietnam, the countries in the region will be at peace... As for the relationship between the commander of this Regiment and a victim of the bloodthirsty people, Xuan Manh just followed the instincts of men who were craving for sexual affection, and maybe he's not unique. On that day, Mong Hung also felt this relationship, but he thought that just like love affairs that suddenly come and go, it is difficult for anyone to be indifferent. But he did not expect that the seed that man had sown on that dead land would grow up into a handsome, fine-looking young man sitting in front of him. Just like the thorny bamboo species in the border area that he mentioned above, the more they are cut down, even burned in the fire, the bigger and stronger shoots they will grow before the vicissitudes of life. Today, those seeds were like bridges connecting the two banks, across the fast-flowing Mekong, for peoples to come together and draw closer together. Chi Tai told him:

After the volunteers withdrew to the country, the remnants of the Pol Pot army took advantage of this opportunity to launch attacks on all fronts. In Siem Reap and Banteay Meanchey, they went to Thma Puok, Svay Chek, Si Sophon and many other places. At Pailin, after invading the town, they rushed down the 10th street, only less than ten kilometers from Battambang town. Many civilians were taken by surprise and did not escape. Members of the reactionary government have entered the town of Pailin, a dream they have had for decades. And then, they just sat there until they were "invited" in front of the bar!

Mong Hung was shocked and was silent for a long time. The image of Ms. Nari reappeared in his mind, he looked directly into Chi Tai's eyes:

- What about the commune women's officer, Ms. Nari?!- He impatiently wants to know the truth. Chi Tai thinks for a moment as if to recall all that happened in the last days before the end of the war, and then tells Uncle Mong Hung:

- After Phearat with half Vietnamese blood was born a few months, Pol Pot soldiers from Pailin attacked the "red land crossroads'. Do you remember the crossroads on 10th street and a branch turning north to get on 58th street? Nari sent the baby to a neighbor who was on the way down to town, and she stayed with the local armed forces to fight against the enemy. Before giving Phearak to a kind person, Nari did not forget to take out the picture from her pocket and put it in the shirt the child was wearing: "If something happens to me, when my child grows up, let him find this man. That's his dad!" Having said that, Nari left right before the Pol Pot soldiers flooded the commune!... And then she and many people fell on the ground that was once stained with the blood of the volunteer soldier!...

Until now, Mong Hung understands everything. He nods his head, looking at the picture again:

- I will help you even though this is not easy, but this is both the responsibility and the feeling of those who care about the love between the two peoples who have long shared the same blood. Children, please rest assured to wait for the day when father and son will be reunited!...

Chapter 25

In the night at the end of the year, it was a bit chilly in the morning in Saigon. At this time, there were only a few lonely cars on the street, occasionally whizzing by under the bright yellow lights from the electric poles. Silent streets with locked front doors were falling asleep after a tiring day in the rapid breathing of urban people. The grandson lying next to Mong Hung turned around, interrupting his train of thought. The boy seemed to know that his grandfather was uneasy about something, he asked:

- Grandpa, why don't you sleep?!

- Go to sleep, you still have class tomorrow morning, this time I don't feel well!

Listening to his words, the boy continued to sleep, the sound of his breathing blowing into his ears was steady, gentle, and he held him in his arms. This year he entered secondary school, his parents went to work far away, sending him back to his grandparents. Lying next to him, Mong Hung's mind wandered, he was unable to fall asleep. For nearly a year now, he had been thinking about the regiment commander of a Regiment that was an obsession for the enemy in the most difficult area in an important strategic direction of the country that had just recovered. Every time he thought about Ngo Xuan Manh, he brought out the picture given to him by Chi Tai and Phearat in Phnom Penh. He had not seen Xuan Manh for thirty years, where is he now? As he got older, his eyes and nose became blurred. He took out his magnifying glass and reviewed every detail of the person in the photo. The more Mong Hung watched, the more suspicious he became: is this exactly Ngo Xuan Manh (?). Thirty years ago, he had a rough, bony face, two protruding cheeckbones that made his eyes always in darkness. Was it due to the life in the rain and sunshine on the battlefield that created that face? When did he take pictures with this woman and that made him look like a young, healthy, handsome young man? At that time, the time when he suspected that he was "sowing seeds" on this land, Mong Hung remembered, at that time, his shaggy hair like a crow's nest had turned gray, with a few silver strands, and his lips were dark, teeth blackened by cigarette smoke. Which meant he's the type who wasn't very handsome. I had seen the picture many times but forgot these details. There was one more thing that disturbed the memoirs of Mong Hung, it is often said: the apple doesn't fall far from the tree. In the other picture, Phearat did not look like Xuan Manh at all, he was more like his mother because of his face, his mother had thick lips like the statue of goddess Absara in Angkor Wat temple. How many self-answered questions were still not satisfactory at all. Or... In this world, there were so many people with the same strange coincidence, the same last name, the same name, the same hometown, was Xuan Manh in this case?...

Thinking of this, Mong Hung got up and dialed the phone number of a friend who had just given him:

- Is it Manh? A friend gave me this number!

- Who's on the other end of the "ine"? What's "rong"?!

- My name is Mong Hung, I seem to have met you somewhere when I was on the Western Front in Cambodia. Was it the years of international duty, your unit operated in Pailin!? - Mong Hung inquired if it was the person he was looking for? The person on the other side seemed to be cautious, making Mong Hung more hopeful.

- Then what do you need from me!

- I apologize in advance if I offend you! - Mong Hung was still very careful about his words, because what he was about to say was extremely personal, many people did not want to make it public, considered it a top secret thing "There's a skeleton in every closet."

- Go ahead, I'll listen!

- I heard that, before withdrawing your troops back home, did you leave a "drop of blood" in Pailin?!...

Mong Hung had a hunch after what he just said, he seemed to be surprised. The other end of the line was silent for a few seconds, and then, seemingly understanding what Mong Hung wants to ask, he answered a question like a completely confident punster:

- Yes, sir, not only a drop but a red "pool" and then seeped into the ground. Damn, luckily I only lost a foot!...

- No! I want to ask if you left a little boy there?!

At this point, Xuan Manh couldn't hold back anymore, he swore, with a Southern accent:

- Fuck you! If I had done what you said, I would be killed by a car on the street a long time ago! - After saying that, Manh hung up the phone with a "bang", an expression as a reaction when his honor was insulted.

Mong Hung regretted, because he was not subtle when he did not know how to use more discreet words, "telling the truth often hurts". But he answered me like that, which means he is a wounded soldier. Not stopping here, Mong Hung rummaged through all the people with the name Manh whose phone numbers he wrote in the "contacts" book, not just commanders or soldiers. It was really "find a needle in a haystack". He looked at the picture again, on the back of the picture was written the word NT, or was Xuan Manh a resident of the Central region, leaving from the coastal city of Nha Trang (NT)? Then during the years of resistance war against invasion and liberation of the country, Nghe An province merged with Ha Tinh, called Nghe Tinh (NT). A few hundred kilometers from Saigon to the North, there is Ninh Thuan province (also NT), or this guy was a resident of the "stayed-in" country, maybe. A ray of hope like a small light had just flashed in the dark night. He went online and contacted Veterans' Associations, first of all in Nghe An province:

- Hi bro! May I ask if you are Ngo Xuan Manh?!
- Mong Hung changed the way of calling so that the listener felt as close as a friend in the same old trench.

- Yes, I'm Manh. Who are you, how do you know me?!

This guy seemed wary, this could be the person I'm looking for:

- I'm Hung, full name is Nguyen Mong Hung, probably the same age as you. I know, you joined the volunteer army, doing international missions to help allied countries in the years 79-80?!

- Thank you for your interest in us volunteer soldiers. District X… two thirds of Veterans are volunteers. I wonder which volunteer army you asked about?!

- I want to know about a person named Ngo Xuan Manh, a Vietnamese volunteer on an international mission in the Cambodian battlefield!

- OH! Then I'm not the one you're looking for. I am also an international volunteer, but on duty in the Laotian battlefield, the fate of people like us has been attached to the history of the two allied countries Laos and Cambodia. There are many veterans on international duty here in Cambodia. If you really need to find it, give me your phone number, the Veterans will meet in a few days, I will give it to you! - Mong Hung heard it, he felt disconcerted, but still have some hope due to the promise of this "near home but far from this alley".

*

It was winter, and it was in a place called "in the middle of nowhere", in addition, the dark clouds were gathering to cover a mountainous area, so it was already dark at six o'clock in the afternoon. Thai Khac Nhu took a flashlight to Manh's house, the two houses were about half a kilometer apart, his friend was famous for being a brave person when he was in Battambang. Thai Khac Nhu and Ngo Xuan Manh lived in the same village, walked this road together from childhood until the day they both enlisted in the army, went to the "K" battlefield together and lived in Battambang, so Nhu was no stranger to this guy, who was handsome and flirted with girls "as sweet as honey".

This afternoon Nhu knew that Manh had just returned from the hospital, Manh was having a sad story, a sadness that couldn't be expressed to anyone other than Thai Khac Nhu: ever since he got married before going to "K" till now his wife hasn't beared any child, now she has a heart disease. "Today I will bring him good news (!)". On the way to Manh's house, Nhu imagined that his friend would be "embarrassed" or overjoyed, perhaps he would jump for joy, but "ashamed", no one knew about this other than me, but me and him are like right hand and left hand. The village road ran along the edge of the stream, frogs called each other to find a place to mate, and Nhu almost stepped on a pair of fire-bellied toads carrying each other across the road.

Seeing the light of the flashlight from the alley sweeping past and shining directly into the house, Manh knew that Nhu was coming:

- You came here at the right time today. I just got back this afternoon. So sad, Nhu! I must have lost the breed. The doctor said: heart disease is associated with joints. They say "That's how joints eat the heart". In times of stress, you will have a stroke, because the heart is also related to blood pressure!... - Manh was talking about his wife.

Nhu looked at his friend's face and smiled, Nhu's half-smile towards Manh at this moment was both uncomfortable and difficult to understand:

- I ask you: Is there a rule of compensation?

Fuck. Why is he asking me this question today? - Manh raised his hand to scratch his head:

- I've been thinking that for a long time and the books say so too! - Manh looked at Nhu's face with suspicion: Why did you ask me this?!

Nhu left the question unanswered, switching to another topic to approach the story he wants to talk about today:

- Does your house still have "spicy water"? Yesterday, I saw you had a bottle of wine with gecko, walrus, how many days have it been soaked? Now you can use it!

Married for a long time, listening to the doctor say that, Manh was very worried. Because he was the first son of the Ngo family, everyone in this village was fat and healthy, although no one said about it, the custom of "heir to the family" of the grandson, the whole family had secretly entrusted to Manh, all these times he did not dare to hold his head high wherever he went because of this "debt" to his ancestors. According to people's words, Manh had found all kinds of folk medicines: which are geckos, coucals, walruses, termite queens, goat testicles, and Korean ginseng, he also brought caught chameleons from the limestone mountains in the border region of the country of pagodas, bordering Thailand, dried them to be supplement, just to get a prince for the Ngo family, but his wife was still consistent, he felt disappointed and felt sorry for her...

- Is there still any wine? - Thai Khac Nhu reminded him. Then bring it here to drink a few cups. I know you are sad, today I will bring you some good news, as the law of compensation is proven here, in your case!...

The day before, Mong Hung searched in his "contacts book" and found a Thai Khac Nhu, long time no see, he was almost buried in the dust of time. On the battlefield, Nhu was a nurse of the 3rd regiment, while Manh was a scout in the Military Intelligence team of Battambang Province. Mong Hung hoped in Nhu. It seemed that this was an arrangement of the law of compensation or something, Nhu said immediately to Mong Hung:

- Manh I know, I know him too well! - Hearing that, Mong Hung thought: maybe this is the person I need to find just like how Chi Tai and Phearat have found me... Thai Khac Nhu told Mong Hung about Manh: "When he was over there, he was often reinforced for the Pailin front. Officers of the 3rd Regiment almost knew him, considering him as the "ears and eyes" of the regimental commander! Under the units, many soldiers thought he was the regiment leader, because there was no important operation without him. He memorized the area of Pailin like the palm of his hand. In 1988, when our troops withdrew to the country, he was kept to carry out "Plan B" at Ally's request. He said to me: "That day I was going to run away with the regiment. You know, I was left without knowing whether I would live or die, the enemy was on all sides, the Pol Pot soldiers in Pailin used to infiltrate the provincial offices, play friendly football matches with me, celebrated the New Year with me, they were so familiar, I stayed here alone, they could kill me any time. I asked him: why don't you run away? It said: I am an officer, a party member, carrying the tradition of a unit that is "trusted by the people, loved by the friends, feared by the enemy", how can I leave. Besides, the people here are so nice, they treat me like their child. I have to close my eyes and hand over my fate to them, relying on the government and people here to finish my mission"! He also has a relationship with Ms.

Nari's sisters, a commune officer, I think that's probably a second reason for him to stay!...

So Mong Hung immediately sent the picture to Thai Khac Nhu.

Without waiting for Xuan Manh to put the wine bottle into two white porcelain "bowls" like two halves of a chicken in the middle of the table, Nhu held a picture of waving in front of Manh:

- Can you guess what this is?!

Seeing a picture with himself in it, Xuan Manh's body seemed to have an electric current running through him, so he put the wine bottle on the table to receive the picture from Nhu's hand. But this guy Nhu was pretty tough, so he pushed Xuan Manh's hand away and put the picture in his chest pocket:

- I have never worked for free for anyone. The stories in the program "Like there was never a separation" on TV, cost billions of dollars. And here, at least a glass first. Fill it up. Let's congratulate you!- The two of them finished their glasses and raised their faces to say "kha" from the back of their throats.

Xuan Manh was not a drunkard. From the day he got married until now, he heard someone say: drinking alcohol can cause impotence, he was afraid of it, so since he returned from the battlefield, he almost quitted drinking. Just had a glass, Xuan Manh's face was already burning, red like a fighting cock. Only then did Nhu show the picture.

Holding the picture in hand, Xuan Manh remembered everything. It was not known whether he was happy or sad, but he suddenly burst out laughing, laughing like never before. That's right, his laughter had stopped since the day his wife got sick, he had been to the hospital twice a day despite the weather, how could he laugh. Now with this special good news, he laughed refreshingly, laughing with tears in his eyes like someone who inhaled "funky balloons". Then he cried and cried like he had never cried before. Perhaps Xuan Manh's inner self now also manifested the "compensation" rule, the time he laughed seemed to be as long as the time he cried. Before his eyes, houses, trees, rivers, animals, and even people were swaying and tumbling. Xuan Manh wanted to say, wanted to scream loudly like a hysterical man, his eyes glittered with tears, his face was stretched and shiny... Thai Khac Nhu was waiting for him to speak, because he thought the words of a drunkard were sincere:

- I'm so glad Nhu. Turns out I'm not an infertile guy, now it's okay to be infertile. I never expected that the days of staying in that place full of traps would give me what not only me but this whole Ngo family is waiting for!... - Xuan Manh brought up the picture again, looking at it for a long time. That's right, that's her. Do you see Phearat as alike as two peas to me? So happy Nhu, I thank you, my Ngo family thank you a thousand times. Today, God tells that you bring me this extremely lucky thing. But Nhu, my happiness is as much as my sadness, because his mother couldn't meet me before she passed away. There is another sadness, you know, my wife now is so poor, so pitiful, if she knows this, she will not be able to bear it, she loves me very much, but women are often like that, many people love their husband, but when they can not give birth a child to her husband's family as she wants, they will become extremely selfish. Perhaps it also comes from the fact that she loves her husband but is afraid of losing her husband, right? To be honest, it's not that I hate my wife now, when living there I sent letters and gifts to encourage her every month. I swear to you, now if it's necessary, I am willing to give half of my heart to my wife, just hope she recovers soon! As for Phearat's mother, I did not expect that in the last few months, before I was ordered to return home, it would become today's story! - Speaking of this, Xuan Manh looked up and stared into Nhu's eyes: "I ask you not to tell anyone but me and you!" Thai Khac Nhu understood his situation:

- You don't thank me for this, I understand too well. The person who, if you have a chance to meet again, you have to thank him, it was Nguyen Mong Hung who sent me this picture, I just have to give it to you! Your happiness is also the happiness of the returning volunteers who were alive!

That night, Xuan Manh told the whole story to his friend. In the sound of frogs calling their group like a harmonious song that whirled into people's hearts and it was sorrowful to the point of being heartbreaking, Thai Khac Nhu just listened and nodded his head:

-   Do you know, after our troops withdrew from the battlefield and returned home, I was assigned to stay and continue to help Ally to strengthen the provincial military intelligence room to maintain the operation to grasp the enemy's situation. Do you remember Miss Nari, that commune official, she had a sister named Bopha, do you know what Bopha means? In Cambodian, Bopha means Rose. She really was a rose, so beautiful Nhu. During the working days there, I was introduced by Nari, at that time, I also thought that her introduction was just a coincidence, just like when acquaintances met, a third person appeared, they were introduced to know each other, that's all. But no wonder Bopha and I gradually had an invisible rope pulling, the two of us getting closer and closer, until there were no longer any obstacles while I was free... Things between me and "Rose" were very long, very personal. It was like many love stories of couples from the past to now, Nari must have known, not only did she not prevent, but she also seemed to encourage the two of us. Then, when today's Pheara was a few months old, there was news that Pol Pot soldiers came down from Pailin after I had an order to return home. And from that day on, I didn't know how the mother and son, and the Bopha sisters were! Thirty years have passed, I thought my "Rose" and Pheara can't live to this day, because I heard that Pol Pot soldiers massacred the people there!

- I understand. In the life of us soldiers, happiness always goes with unhappiness. Your story has a happy ending. Many of us who were left on that land weren't as good as you are now...

About the Author

Nguyen Van Hong

- Full name: Nguyen Van Hong
- Born in July 25, 1945.
- Place of birth: Son Phuc commune, Huong Son district, Ha Tinh province, Vietnam
- Enlisted in the army: 1964.
- Participated in the fight to liberate the South of Vietnam from 1965 - 1975
- Entered the Southwestern border war and international duty in Cambodia: 1979 - 1989.
- Rank: Colonel, now retired.
- Published 11 books
- Member of Ho Chi Minh City Writers' Association
Literary awards:
- First prize, awarded by the Central Newspaper of the Vietnam Veterans Association

-Consolation Prize of the Ministry of Defense for writing about ""Deep memories of Vietnam - Cambodia""
- Awarded by the Vietnam Writers Association of the 2016 - 2020 fiction contest.
- Mekong Literature Prize in 2021."

www.ingramcontent.com/pod-product-compliance
Lightning Source LLC
LaVergne TN
LVHW041700070526
838199LV00045B/1131